D0098924

Dear Reader,

In *Orpheus Girl*, conversion therapy is depicted as the serious human rights violation it is. The book addresses the real and devastating effects that conversion therapy has on those who go through it.

There are scenes in this book that depict self-harm, homophobia, transphobia, and violence against LGBTQ characters. I felt it was necessary to portray the struggles that many members of our community endure in order to raise awareness of the continuing battles we face.

At its core, *Orpheus Girl* is about hope. This is the story of a heroine whose belief in a better future for herself, for the girl she loves, and for the other characters is never shaken. This book is about our community's strength in the face of ignorance, our resilience, and our ability to advocate for a better future for ourselves and for those who come after us.

I hope that Raya's journey inspires you to fight for what you believe in.

—Brynne

Orpheus Girl

Also by Brynne Rebele-Henry

Fleshgraphs

Autobiography of a Wound

ORPHEUS
GIRL

Brynne Rebele-Henry

SOHO
TEEN

Copyright © 2019 Brynne Rebele-Henry

This is a work of fiction. Names, characters, places, and incidents either are the product
of the author's imagination or are used fictitiously, and any resemblance to actual persons,
living or dead, businesses, companies, events, or locales is entirely coincidental.

**Content warning: There are scenes in this book that depict self-harm,
homophobia, transphobia, and violence against LGBTQ characters.**

Published in the United States by Soho Teen
an imprint of Soho Press, Inc.
227 W 17th Street
New York, NY 10011

Library of Congress Cataloging-in-Publication Data
Rebele-Henry, Brynne.
Orpheus girl / Brynne Rebele-Henry.

ISBN 978-1-64129-074-6
eISBN 978-1-64129-075-3

1. Lesbians—Fiction. 2. Best friends—Fiction. 3. Friendship—Fiction.
4. Camps—Fiction. 5. Mythology, Greek—Fiction. 6. Grandmothers—Fiction.
7. Family life—Texas—Fiction. 8. Texas—Fiction. I. Title
PZ7.1.R3975 Orp 2019 | DDC [Fic]—dc23 2019009916

Interior illustration: Freepik.com

Interior design: Janine Agro

Printed in the United States of America

10 9 8 7 6 5 4 3 2 1

Orpheus Girl

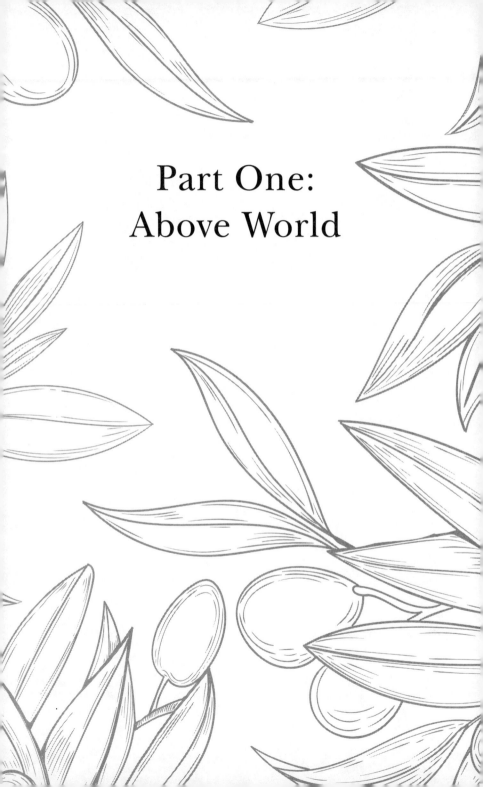

Part One: Above World

Every night Grammy and I watch Mom on the TV. I always thought Mom was a silver screen kind of beauty because of that picture of her in high school: blonde, dimples, all clean-looking. But in this show she's dark-sexy, her hair colored a deep brunette, silky bedsheets held up around her neck with gold ribbons. Mom left Pieria when I was a kid. Grammy would say it was because she needed to go be Aphrodite on the TV. I know that it's because she was tired of it all, of the town and the people. So she disappeared one night. She only told Grammy as she was walking out the door. I was two.

In the car on the way to church this morning, I write Sarah's name in the condensation on the passenger's window, then wipe it off before Grammy can see.

The car is a worn-down blue Volvo from the seventies. It's a miracle it's still running. Every time Grammy slides the key in the ignition and it actually starts, she thanks God under her breath. The seat belts are frayed so much that they could snap if you pulled too hard, so we stopped using them. I have to hold onto the car door to keep from falling out of my seat every time Grammy brakes. She drives like a maniac. Runs over mailboxes on a regular basis, hits curbs, mows down shrubs. Once she ran over an abandoned lemonade stand. She never stops to deal with what she's run over, just keeps going, like she's late on her way to somewhere really important.

I get through the service like I always do: running myths through my head. Ever since I found my mom playing Aphrodite on that soap opera, I've been memorizing them. I know it's stupid, but I've always thought that one day I'll open the door and she'll be there, and I'll need something to talk about. And since my mom's Aphrodite, I might as well be able to talk about myths. During the service I think about Persephone, how the girl was pulled away from everything she'd ever known and taken to a strange world. Or Atalanta. In these myths, girls are always being changed or taken by men, their voices, their protests ignored. And the queer girls, like Atalanta, are forced to become something else.

Grammy's always talking about how one day I'll have a normal life, with a husband and two kids (a boy and a girl) and a brick house with a white picket fence and a big yellow dog who'll run around the yard. She says my husband should work so I don't have to, and I'll stay home all day and make cookies the way she taught me and go to PTA meetings and church. Whenever she talks about it, she gets a misty look in her eyes and twists the gold chain of her cross necklace between her fingers, and I know it's not my life she's imagining, that secretly she's wondering what would have happened if her own husband hadn't died in a car accident at twenty-seven and left her with a two-year-old girl, if her girl hadn't gotten pregnant senior year of high school only to run off three years later.

Instead, she still has a job arranging and delivering flowers for weddings and funerals and baptisms, continual reminders of her own wedding and her husband's service, and she makes me go to cotillions and dance with boys, refuses to let me wear pants to school, and makes me go to church three times a week and Bible camp in the summer and try out for cheerleading every August.

Every fall since fourth grade, she's bought me a new pair of shiny green pom-poms. She takes the day off work to come to the tryouts with me. I walk into the gym with a lump in my throat, but I never can kick high enough or land lightly enough, and every year we drive home together in disappointed silence. When we get home, Grammy always says she has a "headache worse than Satan," and she goes upstairs to lie down and change out of the "Go Team!" sweatshirt she wears just for tryouts. We both know that her head's not hurting, that she just doesn't want to have to pretend not to be let down yet again, but I always nod and don't say anything.

This year, before she went upstairs, she said, "You were supposed to be my second chance." But she said it so quietly I think I wasn't supposed to hear her.

Since then we've never talked about tryouts again. I think maybe she finally just gave up.

冊 冊 冊

ONCE THE service ends, I heap pastries and the little watercress-and-pickle and peanut-butter tea sandwiches that the church ladies make onto my plate, then sit down on the coffee-stained couch outside Preacher Sam's office and eat until I feel sick. Every time I go to Sarah's dad's church I get this sinking feeling, like something's wrong with me and if they find out, when they find out, it's all over.

Most nights I dream that Sarah and the choir boys and Preacher Sam are peering down at me. I'm wearing another girl's clothes but I don't know why. When Preacher Sam hands me a crucifix, my skin starts burning and wings burst out of my back, and I'm trying to get the wings to stop sprouting from my back but they won't, and soon I'm screaming and burning and they're whispering "freak" and then they're yelling it.

The dreams started when I was eight, shortly after I realized I was different from the girls I went to school with, but I didn't yet know how, just that there was some strange and invisible barrier separating me from them. Often, at after-school church camp, I'd watch the girls running around, skipping rope or drawing on the pavement outside the church, and my back would ache for reasons I could never discern. On those days, I tried to pinpoint the difference, the thing separating me, causing me to feel like every movement I made was an act, a dream that I would wake up from, like a fortune-teller sifting her tea leaves, trying to gather together some foreign objects and principles into a crystalline answer. But for years the bowl would come back empty, nothing more than water and stray oolong straining to reach the surface.

When I was born, I had two small, misplaced vertebrae sticking out of my back. They looked like wings. The doctors took pictures, then set the vertebrae back in place. Now I just have two bumps and a line of scars on my back. Sometimes at night, I run my fingers over the bumps, try to imagine what the wings would have looked like. The doctors made the first incision in my vertebrae, so the worst of the scars are low on my back, though the scar tissue maps all the way up to my shoulders in a messy sprawl. The doctors said I healed better than expected. They'd thought I'd be disfigured. But I just don't wear bikinis like the other girls, always make sure my tops don't slip down past my shoulder blades. I don't need anyone else thinking about my being different even more than they already do. I don't want to cause any suspicion—at least not any more suspicion than being motherless in a little town already creates.

The only time that Grammy ever acknowledged my scars was once when I was ten. I was standing in front of the bathroom mirror staring at the faded-to-pale lines, watching the ruined skin ripple when I moved. I remember trying not to cry when I saw how ugly it was, how the marks of what was once a wound, a defect, covered me. I'd never paid much notice to the scars before, had always just considered them a part of me, normal, but the day before, Sarah and I had gone swimming, and when she'd crouched at the edge of the pool before diving in, I saw the smooth stretch of her back, her unscarred shoulders, the skin taut and gold from the sun, and a hard lump of something akin to shame worked its way into my throat and made it hard to swallow.

Later that night, alone in the house, I prepared to try to find a way to make myself beautiful too, to try to rid myself of the ruined thing inside of me—the constant gnawing feeling that I was hiding something, that some part of my girlhood, and my body itself, was defective, wrong. But there was no way to get rid of the scars, no way to remove the proof that I was different than the other, unmarred girls I grew up with.

I remember clawing at the scars, as if I could scrape the ugliness away, as if I could cleanse it out of myself from the outside in. When that didn't work, I scrubbed at my back with a washcloth I'd covered with dish soap. I was getting hysterical by then, my face screwed up with panic. My skin was flushed with shame and I was crying so hard that I didn't hear her come in, but when I looked up she was in the doorway, watching.

Grammy knelt down on the bathroom floor so that we were at eye level, and she grabbed both of my hands in hers. My fingers were bloody from scratching the skin around the scars, and the blood smeared into a faint red on her palms. She stared at me for a minute, like she was trying to remember something she hadn't recalled for years, and then she cleared her throat. "Raya, this is God's doing. He makes everything in his image, you know. And so he gave you these wings, like an angel. You know, when you were born, the parts of your back they had to take out looked just like a baby bird's. He made you in his image; he made you like him. And you need to accept that."

Though I never put much weight in God, from then on, whenever I saw the scars, that feeling of disgust that had always risen up in my mouth like bile whenever I saw my body was replaced with a kind of grudging acceptance: Grammy said they were beautiful, that I was marked for some reason, that maybe my being here wasn't as much of an accident as I'd always felt like it was, and I thought that maybe that could be enough.

囧 囧 囧

NOW, AT church, Grammy is talking to Mr. Paul. A widower. He's got two grown girls and a boy in college. She's flushed and, I notice, she's put on lipstick. It's the first time I've seen her wear it in years. The lipstick has smeared off on her front teeth, leaving a red streak. Sarah appears at my side so I sidle up to them, crossing my legs then uncrossing them again, as if I'm so impatient for her to leave that it's making me piss myself.

Grammy notices. "Raya, go get more banana bread."

I shuffle off, ignoring Sarah even when she sticks her tongue out at me.

Ever since Rosie from our school saw her kiss me, I've been avoiding Sarah, saying it's because it's summer and I'm busy keeping Grammy company. I remind her that it's August, the month that Grandpa died all those years ago. Grammy doesn't sleep so well, just stays up late and listens to the cicadas shrill their last mating calls of the season. But we both know the reason is because we got found out. I tell myself we weren't doing anything real. Sarah was just practicing for Bryce, the boy she pretends she likes when other girls ask who her crush is, the boy she'll probably date until she gets out of here, goes to the Bible college in Houston that her dad went to.

Rosie screeched when she saw us, her lips a tight white line and hands clenched into shaking fists.

Later that day Sarah put her hands on my back, and I know she felt the wing-bumps because her eyes got wide, but she didn't say anything. She'd seen them before, of course, despite my trying to keep her from noticing, twisting my back when I changed in front of her in an attempt to hide them, but she'd never touched them before, had never felt the ridges of scar tissue that mark my back like a messy landscape—terrain that even I, after all this time, have a hard time bringing myself to feel.

Sarah finally corners me outside the church, in the backyard. "Raya?"

"Yeah, what is it?"

"Are you ignoring me?" She narrows her eyes. "Because we didn't do anything wrong."

I look around, make sure no one's watching. "Yeah, we did."

"What did we do?"

"Rosie saw us."

She flushes. "We were just pretending."

"That's what I told her."

She shrugs. "Then we're not in trouble."

I see Grammy walking up to me. Her cheeks are pink. She's holding a card with what looks like a phone number written on it.

"Okay, kiddo."

Sarah puts on her best Good Girl smile, shifts her weight onto one hip. "Hi, Mrs. Lewis."

She grins. "Hi, Sarah. You should come over later. I'll

make my famous bread pudding. You know, Raya's birthday is coming up soon too."

"I'd like that."

"Of course. Come over any time you like, hon."

"Thanks. I will." She gives me a look, the same look she gave me that day under the bleachers at school, about a few minutes before Rosie stopped us, but it was already too late. We were already gone.

⊞ ⊞ ⊞

BACK HOME I flip through the tapes, watch Mom reruns. In every episode she looks a little different. In my favorite one, her eyes are sparkling and green and she has this sort of triumph in them. In last week's show, they were bloodshot. This week she looks pretty but cold, her eyes rimmed with pink, like she's been crying. But maybe it's just the television makeup. Maybe she's just supposed to look sad.

I don't remember anything about Mom except the day she left, even though I'm probably too young to remember it. She was holding a suitcase, and in the dying light I swear she had some kind of halo. Grammy was standing in the door and she called out her name, Calli, but she didn't look back. Then she was gone.

Sometimes I think it was a dream, that Mom never really existed at all. But then I remember Grammy's sadness. It's a quiet kind of sadness, but still, it's there. You can see it in the way she hunches her shoulders into themselves, like she's trying to disappear inside her own body.

⊞ ⊞ ⊞

I'M IN the living room alone when the door opens.

Sarah lets herself in like it's her house. "Hey."

"Hi."

"I wanted to talk to you about that day."

"Okay."

She sits next to me on the couch. She's still wearing her Sunday school dress, pink with small pearl buttons. Her parents choose her church clothes for her, with the unspoken agreement that if she wears their frilly femme dresses three times a week, she can be as butch as she wants on non-church days, can wear boys' clothes and wash her face clean of makeup. They don't say anything, just talk about how she's such a tomboy, that she needs to go with a nice boy, is all.

Our friendship had always existed in a precarious balance of secretly knowing what the other person is but never acknowledging it.

Instead we would talk about the boys in our school, trying to convince each other that we might one day actually be interested in them, parsing together fake stories about boys we didn't know and didn't want to know. We would tell them in whispers, as if performing the rite enough times would make our words true and we would become the girls in our stories about ourselves. At least we used to do that. After this summer I think we both gave up a little bit, because the hushed stories stopped.

When she kissed me, her tongue was warmer than I thought it would be, and her hands were shaking, though only a little bit.

She opens her mouth and starts to say something, but then she closes it again.

I stir uncomfortably. "Well?"

"I wasn't pretending."

I can feel my face flushing. "What do you mean?" I give her a look like, *This is your chance to be able to take it all back, to pretend we're like the other girls,* but instead she lunges forward and kisses me again.

I hear Grammy gasp. She's dropped the pudding bowl.

I don't know what she saw or what I can say, so I do something stupid. I run. I run out the door and into the street, and I don't stop running until I reach the convenience store on the corner. I skid into the store, panting. I keep thinking, *This is it; it finally happened.* My heart's beating too fast and I can feel my knees going weak. Miss Shirley, the owner, stares at me, so I buy a bag of taffy with the last quarter in my pocket. I sit outside the store and chew until my teeth hurt. Years ago I learned to do what Grammy does, which is to eat sugar whenever there's a void inside myself that needs to be filled, to spoon sugar straight from the bowl into my mouth, to let the stuff dissolve on my tongue, leaving only the residue of that particular sadness. But this time it just makes me feel queasy, so I throw the rest of the taffy away and walk home.

※ ※ ※

WHEN I get back, Grammy's sitting at the kitchen table, smoking a cigarette, something I've never seen her do. I didn't even know she had cigarettes. She looks different, older. I can see all the wrinkles in her face but, more than that, how tired she looks. Like she's ancient. It strikes me then that I've never known Grammy as anything other than an old woman with an absentee daughter, that we've never known each other as anything more than two people who were abandoned by the same person. Despite the fact that she raised me, to her I'm no more than the straight granddaughter she had to raise, and she's always been my sad Grammy who's had to work extra to support us both, who has permanent worry lines and who can never make it through a full movie without falling asleep even though she pretends she's never really tired.

I step into the kitchen, sit down next to her. "Grams?"

She looks at me like she doesn't even recognize me. "Sarah's upstairs."

"We were just pretending."

"You're both too old for that."

"But we weren't doing anything, really."

She sighs.

"Sarah just likes this boy, Bryce, you know," I tell her. "Wanted to practice for him. I didn't want her to. Thought it was a bad idea."

Grammy puts a hand on my shoulder. She doesn't say anything, just keeps smoking. Then she nods at me. Her face has relaxed. I only realize the tension was there after it's gone. I breathe a sigh of relief, like I escaped something terrible, though I don't know what I have escaped exactly, or what she would have done had she really found out everything.

᠁ ᠁ ᠁

I FIND Sarah sitting on my bed, her eyes red and sore-looking. She won't look at me.

When I spend the night at Sarah's, her parents always make frozen dinners and then Sarah and I, until a couple of years ago, would take baths together, wash each other's hair. Whenever I saw her like that, in the bath, I'd get a sharp feeling in my stomach, try to look away so I wouldn't see her naked body. Sometimes I'd notice her watching me through her veil of hair, a blush slowly spreading down her face, though neither of us ever acknowledged it, so I could almost convince myself that I was only imagining it, that it didn't mean anything.

I didn't know what it meant back then, that hot rush in my belly and lower, but I knew I wasn't supposed to have it. Then, the year that we stopped taking baths together, I learned what that feeling in my stomach meant. I hooked up with a few girls in secret, didn't tell her about it.

One night in her bed, the first time I suggested we take separate baths, she put her hand in between my legs. She didn't do anything, just rested it there. Then she took her hand away. We never talked about it, and she never did it again.

Sarah, like me, is almost always alone. But unlike me, both her parents live together, and she has a brother, John. But she didn't like them, didn't like how her daddy was always preaching and making her wear dresses and go to church for every service. Sometimes she used to say she wished she had only a grandma like me, but I guess once she got to know me better and learned about the sadness of living almost alone, she changed her mind, because she doesn't say that anymore.

I'd often go to church with her and we'd whisper during service, giggling while the Sunday school kids shushed us. At school she was the bigger half of my only two friends. My other friend was Rosie, who, since she saw whatever happened that day, won't speak to me and gets pink-faced whenever I try to talk to her. Sometimes when I see Sarah, I feel something like love twisting in my throat, but I always push it back down, try to swallow it. I never thought that she could love me, that any girl would. Whenever I thought about my future, it seemed like nothing more than an empty slate. The only certain thing I could ever think of for myself is the promise that one day I'll be caught, that one day, just like all the other girls like me, I'll disappear.

☷   ☷   ☷

NOW, UPSTAIRS in my room, Sarah is twisting her coppery gold hair between two fingers, her face all crumpled up. It takes me a minute to realize she's crying, that she's shaking a little bit too, like the first time we kissed, only now her whole body is trembling.

"Sarah?"

"I need to tell you something."

"Okay."

She gets up and closes the door with a soft click, slides the lock, then comes back and sits next to me.

"It wasn't the first time I did that."

She's crying harder, the mascara her mom makes her wear streaking down her cheeks, leaving black trails on her skin.

"It wasn't for me either."

☷   ☷   ☷

THE SUMMER before, at Bible camp, a girl named Jean and I got locked in the crafts supply closet. In the two hours it had taken for a teacher to come find us, we'd explored each other's mouths and I'd let her push up my shirt and run her hands over what were not quite breasts but weren't nothing either. She stopped before the counselor found us. The counselor's name was LeAnne, and she had six kids in the program and seemed perpetually dissatisfied with something. Thankfully she didn't seem to notice that my shirt was half-off, just told us to get the dried corn skeins to the students for their crosses.

Jean was like some kind of Artemis, a gay girl warrior. She was fifteen, and she lived on a farm-like commune with her four parents and drove a tractor around like it was a car. She had catlike cheekbones and a shaved head. She smoked a lot of weed and always smelled like some kind of strange smoke that left her voice scratchy. I don't know why she was at church camp since her parents were real hippies, polyamorists. But I guess that, like me, she just needed something to do in our dried-up town, didn't want to spend all her days smoking on her farm or helping her parents grow flowers and raise chickens.

It's a wonder our town didn't revolt at her family's presence, given that last year on prom night a girl got found with another girl, and she was sent away by her parents to a boarding school in California, never heard from again. I don't know what happened to the other girl, nobody ever saw her after that night, when the principal opened the door and saw her with her arms around the other girl, her flame-red hair coming out of its braid. Her carnation corsage's petals were probably crushed on the closet floor. The theme was *Under the Sea* and their satin mermaid-tail dresses were half-ripped, the strawberry scented body glitter they'd painted on their cheeks like scales were smeared into ugly pink streaks.

I guess their disappearances show that being gay here is considered more offensive than any other sin, which is why I haven't tried to tell anyone about myself. I already know what would happen, and I don't want to disappear, too.

Jean was homeschooled, so I never saw her again after summer ended. Once I thought I saw a girl who looked like her walking down to the river, but when I called Jean's name, the girl didn't turn. When I ran up to her, I saw that it wasn't her at all. I think I thought that maybe I could love her, but I never got to find out. Maybe I just wanted to think about someone other than Sarah.

The only time I went over to Jean's house, she was stretched out on a hay bale in the barn like a panther, smoking. She offered me some of her joint. I managed to take two hits before I started coughing my lungs out. I'd never done anything like that before, but I thought I might as well, that it didn't really matter anymore with everything else we were doing. Things got kind of hazy. Then we were kissing and hay was everywhere. Then she was on top of me, running her fingers up my thighs. But that was all we did because I started getting nervous and couldn't stop coughing. I thought maybe someone was watching us and knew what we'd done and would tell everyone. I started crying and Jean obviously didn't know what to do because she just sat there silently looking at her hands until I stopped.

Afterward she tried to feed me some oatmeal bars that her mom had baked, but I started crying again because even though I never got to know her, I still missed my own mother. Eventually Jean just piled the hay around me like a blanket and ambled off to smoke another joint. I fell asleep, and when I woke up, it was dark and I still felt high. I got upset again and demanded that she take me the seven miles home in the dark. Jean sighed, then climbed into the John Deere tractor she used as a car and floored it.

Jean got distracted and started driving in loops around the school parking lot until we realized we were driving in circles and not to my house. We parked the tractor down the road so Grammy wouldn't see it.

When I got home, I told Grammy that I had been at Sarah's with Sarah and Jean and that we had been working on something for church camp but it was too late for Jean to drive back. Then I ran upstairs before she could smell the smoke on my clothes and in my hair or see my bloodshot eyes.

I doused my shirt and Jean's in the rose-scented Febreze that Grammy buys in bulk, sprayed the perfume Grammy had bought me for my fifteenth birthday into my hair. Jean fell asleep in my bed with her arm around my shoulders, but the next morning when I woke up, she was gone and that was the last time I ever saw her. I wanted to tell Sarah, but I never did. I was scared that if I told her what had previously been unspoken, then everything we'd quietly built together over the years would fall apart.

🔠 🔠 🔠

WHEN SHE'S done crying, Sarah laughs kind of sadly. "Are you"—here she gestures in the space between us—"you know, too?"

I swallow. If I say it out loud, it will be the first time I've told anyone. With Jean I cried not because she knew, but because I didn't have to tell her.

"Yeah. I am."

She's got a weird look on her face, the same way that I've seen different kinds of girls look at the leading man right after he pulls them out of burning buildings in the old black-and-white movies Grammy makes me watch with her on Friday nights, the same movies that Grammy never stays awake long enough to finish. Then she puts her arms around my shoulders and kisses me in a way I wasn't expecting, and I kiss her back in a way I didn't think I could. And this time, neither of us needs to say anything to pretend that this isn't right. After, she falls asleep with her head on my chest and I hold her so tightly I can feel her heart beating against my rib cage.

🏮 🏮 🏮

IT'S ALMOST midnight. I'll be sixteen in three minutes. I hate my birthdays because even though I know it's stupid, every birthday I think Mom is going to come back to see me, or at least call me. I can't remember a time when I didn't spend my birthdays with a sick and kind of excited feeling in my stomach. I always brush my hair out really good so that the curls lie flat. And every time the phone rings I jump, feel like I'm going to throw up, even though I know in my bones it's not going to be her. And it never is. I don't know how to miss someone I never knew, but I do. I like to think that one day I'll go out to L.A. to find her. But I know she doesn't want to be found.

Sometimes I buy something stupid and pretend it's from her. This year it's either going to be a bottle of glittery daisy-yellow nail polish or a pack of Wrigley's. Something else I do on all of my birthdays: I take out the shoebox where I keep the only things she left behind for me. There's a half-empty perfume bottle with a crack in the side. Her hairbrush: a few strands of black hair mingle in with the blonde from the time she dyed her hair the wrong shade. There's a photo of us on the day I was born, the only photo of us together that I've ever seen, the only thing I have that proves that Grammy and I didn't dream her up. It's held together by layers of scotch tape. I'm afraid that one day it will fall apart completely and I won't be able to put it back together again. And then I won't have anything else to remember her by.

Twice every year (on my birthday and on Mom's birthday), I uncork the bottle to smell the remnants of her old perfume, try to use that scent to deduce something about her, what she was like. In the box there are also two photos of Mom in high school, the only ones she didn't take with her. In the pictures she's sunny and blonde and smiling. She looks different from the other girls, though. Older. Like she knows things none of them do. Like she came from another time.

She has sharp cheekbones and a high forehead with big, almost-blue eyes and a Byzantine nose, full lips that turn down at the corners, long straight blonde hair. I got everything but the hair. Mine's wild and curly and the same black as the shale that washes up on the riverbank. In the pictures Mom doesn't look happy. She looks like she could have been a different person, like she didn't know what her life would become or that she'd get pregnant a few months after both pictures were taken. That she'd leave me. That in a few years she'd be a starlet with sad eyes playing a half-naked Aphrodite on TV. Last year I tried to find her. I knew it was stupid, but when I googled her I thought maybe I could find an address, a number I could call. But all I found were pictures of Mom smiling emptily and some gossip columns.

The last thing of hers that I have is an old bracelet made out of dingy plastic pearls. Sometimes I slide it on my wrist, but it always leaves a green tinge on my arm. It's my favorite thing of hers. I like to imagine where she got it. Sometimes I pretend that my father gave it to her, that maybe that's why she left it behind: so I'd have something from him. But considering the things that Grammy's said, I know that my father, like me, was probably someone she never stuck with long enough to know or keep.

I hold each item carefully, like they're relics from another world. Every time I look in the box, I find out something new about her, notice another almost-microscopic difference in her things. Once I noticed that a small yellow thread from something was wrapped around her hairbrush. Another time I found a small dried-up clover pressed beneath her cheerleading trophy. I couldn't figure out what that meant, eventually decided that she'd probably put the trophy down in a field, that the flower stuck and she never noticed.

I always wonder if Mom actually wanted to be a cheerleader, or if she just did it so that Grammy would look at her the way she looks at me when I put on the cheerleading uniform and awkwardly hold up my pom-poms, if Mom was ever really any of the things that Grammy likes to say she was, or if it was all just Grammy trying to change her into the girl she always wanted the both of us to be.

⌗ ⌗ ⌗

SARAH STIRS in her sleep, puts a hand on my chest. I can see her eyes flicker open, but then she squeezes them tight, pretends to still be sleeping. I pull her closer. She smells like the vanilla extract she dabs on her pulse points every morning. I don't know why she does that instead of buying regular perfume, but she does, and somehow when the vanilla mixes with the scent of her skin, it becomes strange and exotic. Like a hothouse flower so rare no one except her has found it before.

I fall asleep and dream about the wings bursting from my back again, the faces of the choir singers peering down at me. In the dream it's like I've changed so much they can't even recognize me, like I've morphed into something beyond remembering. I wake up gasping. Sometimes when I'm afraid of my future here, on nights like these when I try to sleep but only have nightmares, I think of Odysseus sailing uncharted seas, fighting to find his home again. I pretend I'm only sailing through Pieria, that I have another home to return to.

⌘ ⌘ ⌘

WHEN I wake up, Sarah is watching me with an odd look on her face, something between desire and sadness. Her cheek has a mark from where the button on my shirt was pressing into her face, and her lips are turned down with sleep. I sit up, push her off me as gently as I can.

She laughs a little bit. "Hey stranger."

"Hey yourself."

She kisses me, and even though I was expecting it, the

kiss still feels like some kind of revelation. We stay like this, her mouth on mine, my arms around her, until the sun rises and the light casts shadows like waves over our bodies.

Downstairs Grammy has set the table with her favorite table-cloth (purple with crosses in the fabric) and put a vase filled with red roses in the center of it. She's made her banana waffles, a semisecret recipe that takes a pound of sugar. She's inordinately proud of these waffles and makes them on every holiday, minor or major. Grammy eyes Sarah, like she knows something she doesn't want to, but she doesn't say anything.

When Sarah's parents ring the doorbell to take her home, she pulls me back upstairs, telling Grammy that she forgot to give me my birthday card.

She gives me a short, fast kiss, like she's trying to work something out on me with her mouth. I don't mind. I try to wipe the just-kissed look off my face and walk her out the door. I watch the car disappear, until it's nothing more than a blue speck on the horizon and the dust it kicked up has settled, leaving only the smell of exhaust and tire tracks in our dried-up dirt driveway.

Grammy cooks for half the day, says we have a special guest, but she won't tell me who. I've already guessed, though: Mr. Paul. Or my mom. But really, I know it's just going to be Paul. I try to remind myself not to get my hopes up like I have every year since I can remember. I think Grammy's going to start seeing Paul. He is the only widower in town. I heard at church that every Friday he goes into the woods and shoots birds. Nobody knows what he does with them once he kills them, just that he kills them. I think maybe he's trying to feel in control of death, since his wife died in that car crash. I heard someone else say that he was in the crash too, that he escaped with only a few broken ribs and has blamed himself ever since.

But that story could just be a small town rumor, which in Pieria is when a not very interesting or particularly true story about someone in the town gets turned into a myth of epic proportions, just because everyone knows each other and their cousins and their parents before them so well that they'd go crazy if they didn't believe something strange and interesting was going down. Like the tale about the mayor's wife being the secret daughter of James Joyce, first spread in the summer of 2004 and now accepted as a fact by everyone (except the wife). Or the story about my father being a criminal nicknamed Pollo, on the lam for robbing four banks in Austin, which has been going around for longer than I can remember. It's unfair since I never met my father, don't even know his name, and probably never will. Grammy thinks he's one of the football players from Mom's senior class.

Later, when Grammy's out helping Paul with some kind of ambiguous "church thang," I climb the rickety stairs to the third floor.

Sometimes, when Grammy is working, I like to sit in Mom's room and try to remember things about her. All my memories of her are so hazy that often I think I made them up, but I guess I'll never know. Before Grammy comes home, I always go through the room and make sure everything is exactly where Mom left it before I slip downstairs, pretend to have been at the dining room table doing my homework.

Her room is painted pale blue, and there are little baskets filled with Beanie Babies hanging over her bed. She painted clouds on her ceiling so it looks like the sky. Her bed is white, with a pink canopy over it. Then there's a wooden crib from when she was a baby that Grammy gave her after my birth. There's a tube of Wet n Wild lipstick in Creative Cranberry on the yellow dresser. There's also a cracked mirror, a rainbow carpet, and a rocking chair missing an arm, but that's it.

After Mom left, Grammy kept the room exactly the same, like a shrine, as if one day Mom would come back and expect everything to be how she left it. Once every couple of months she dusts it, but other than that, the door to her room stays closed.

I take one of Mom's smaller cheerleading trophies off the wall and hold it, try to imagine what she was like all those years ago. Sometimes I wonder what things would be like if she'd stayed, if she'd ever gotten a chance to know me.

After, I go through everything else in the box. I let myself take the picture of us out again, but just for a little bit. In the picture I'd just been born, was nothing more than a little red dot of a baby with a bandage where my vertebrae wings were, and Mom was exhausted but beautiful. Her sunflower-like hair was a messy halo around her tear-stained face. Instead of wearing a hospital gown, she'd brought her own robe: pale pink with red stripes that matched her mouth and her cheeks perfectly.

When Grammy gave me the photo for the first time, she sighed sadly and said, "You look just like her." The way she said it, it didn't sound like a good thing, and the sour tone of her voice stayed with me long after I'd begun to make myself forget about what she'd said.

Next I take out the empty bottle of her favorite perfume. It's by Guess, a brand I've never seen anywhere except for in the glossy magazines the rich girls at school have. The magazines get passed around, from the popular to the unpopular, until they work their way down to Sarah and me, and by then the clothes will already be out of season. Whenever I look at the girls in the magazines, a strange hunger rises up in my throat: a hunger for the kind of girl I'll never be.

Sarah and I never needed to tell each other why we'd pore over those magazines. I always knew that she, too, was researching how straight girls dress and talk, how they arrange their expressions for the camera. Sometimes, without saying anything, she and I would practice their poses in front of the mirror. Hold our hands at a tilt in front of our stomachs like Barbies. Try jutting our hips out and hooking our thumbs through our belt loops, making an expression somewhere between a smile and a snarl. I saw her doing the Barbie wave at church one day, and then I started doing it too.

Mom's perfume smells like stale roses and cinnamon, something else smoky and foreign that leaves my throat feeling scratchy. I found it in her dresser one day, when I was poking around her old room and trying to remember what she was like.

Once I saw Grammy walking up to the third floor with a box, I guess to pack up some of Mom's things. But once she got to the top of the stairs, she turned around and walked away without even opening the door. Before she went outside, I saw her wipe her eyes with the end of a dish towel. Then she left "to get some fresh air" and didn't come back until it was dark. Her eyes were red, and she looked sadder than she'd let herself look for a long time. Grammy's grief is mostly hidden, though when she does let it show, it's so intense I worry it's breaking her open from the inside, like that day when the shell of the hard woman she became was split open to reveal her raw and trembling fleshy core, its messy pink heart.

⊞ ⊞ ⊞

I SLIP out of Mom's room only when I hear Grammy slam the door, and Paul's voice, then the sizzling of food. I go back downstairs. I try to seem sullen when Paul hands me more flowers, yellow carnations, while Grammy beams. Really I'm happy for her, if not for myself. While the widower is interesting in an anthropological way, I don't want him in my house, dating my grandmother. I want to keep going the way we have been all these years, when it's just us, both lonely and unattached and floating around the house like ghosts, two people who don't really belong to anybody, only tenuously belong to each other, our relationship based on little more than misfortune.

And while sometimes I wonder if she knew if she would still love me, or if Grammy ever even wanted me, our mutual sadness is better than pretending to be a little family, pretending that we both chose this, that in her absence we're not just drifting, not spending our time together in mutual denial, just waiting for her to return, even though we both know she's not going to.

Tonight Grammy's made more food than the three of us can eat, but I'm starving for something I can't explain. I try to eat, but it feels like I'm hosting some insatiable hunger inside me that nothing can fill.

🔲 🔲 🔲

THE NEXT morning it's Monday, and Mondays I always sleep over at Sarah's while Grammy pulls a late shift arranging the week's new shipment of flowers—preserving and freezing each pale pink lily, each yellow tulip, so that it'll stay fresh for the rest of the week.

I wash and brush my hair. I line my eyes with an eyeliner that I burned the tip of with a cigarette lighter, wing the liner so my eyes are all catlike and obsidian, like those jet-black rocks I sometimes find by the river, the ones that used to be chiseled into arrows or knives. The more popular boys carve theirs into arrowheads and loop twine through the hole, wear them like necklaces, and in the summer when the rocks catch the sun and get hot, it burns their skin, but they keep them on, don't take them off until the necklaces themselves break, leaving behind a triangle of pale skin in the place the arrowhead was.

In the mirror I look mythic. Like I could be on TV with Mom. I look like the girl who played a young Orpheus before he died. So in love. But also, so tragic. Grammy couldn't tell that the actor was gay, but I could. Being queer gives you some kind of insight into other queers. I can sense them in my presence like the gods in the myths could find other deities, like Jean did with me that day at church camp. A sixth sense almost.

I put on the red baby doll top with "Girl Power!" printed on it, one of the long purple peasant skirts with mirrors stitched into them that Grammy keeps buying for me. She thinks that if she keeps forcing me to wear ladylike clothes, then the parts of me that are like my mom that she sees growing inside of me will disappear. Like she can flatten them out the same way she presses corsages between two sheets of plastic to preserve the flowers after they've been used and discarded. She lays them out in little glass boxes and gives them back to their original owners for a price. Sometimes, at other girls' houses, I'll see the boxes displayed on their mantels or dressers, and I'll think of her on all those early mornings, trying to save those girls' memories so that they don't have to worry about trying to hold onto them themselves.

Grammy is already gone. I burn the leftover waffles, miss the bus. I think about eating but instead drink yesterday's coffee, so thick it tastes like dirt. It leaves a greasy residue in my throat that I know I will prod for the rest of the day. I walk to school with the bitter aftertaste still on my tongue.

Rosie is the first person I see when I arrive. I feel a twinge of fear when I realize she still won't look at me. She's smacking her Bubblicious, and it makes a sugary congealed sound as it hits her gums. Her feathered blonde hair has been scraped into a too-tight ponytail, and she's wearing a pair of the hot pink bedazzled cowboy boots that all the cheerleaders bought after making the squad. I can feel her eyes burning into the back of my neck when I turn away.

Everything the popular girls wear is coated in a thin layer of plastic or glitter, like a drugstore candy. Sometimes I think that the girls themselves are made out of plastic. All the popular girls have blonde highlights like streaks of snow or butter. While the color of the highlights changes depending on the girl, they're all done with the same hair dye at the same sleepovers. They wear frosty blue eyeshadow and either the bubblegum pink Lancôme Juicy Tubes or MAC's brick-red Lipglass. They have names like Helenie or Pandora. The most popular calls herself Peneloppe, with two *p*'s. They buy their clothes from Delia's catalogs and date only football players.

Sometimes when I look at these girls, I see both what my mom might have been like and what I could have been, if I wasn't spending all my waking hours worrying that I was walking wrong, that I looked at another girl in the hall for too long, that no matter how hard I try to hide it, they can tell anyway, that they'll still find out somehow. My first day of school, I tried to talk to the more popular girls, thought that maybe if they inducted me into their clique, then I could pass through school safely without much questioning: their approval would be the only thing I'd need to stay hidden, to keep anyone from thinking too much for too long about me. But it didn't work, and when I sat down next to them during lunch, they all got up from the table and left, leaving me alone and crimson-faced as the whole cafeteria watched.

Sometimes I wonder how it will happen, if one day I'll be found with another girl, or if it will be a quieter kind of outing. If maybe I'll look at a girl and flush too red, if it will be because I rejected another boy, never went on a single date. Maybe it will be the way I move, because I can't make my hips swing the same way as the straight girls can. Maybe they'll just be able to tell that everything I wear, the makeup and hairstyles and dresses, is a costume because of how stiff I feel inside the identity that's been chosen for me. Or maybe one day someone here will look at me and just know and that will be it.

The girls rim their eyes with blue, and their lips are like melting Popsicles; their makeup is always both overlined and almost imperceptibly skewed. I think of Paul as I watch them, imagining that this is the way he probably watches those birds when he goes hunting: hungry, but distant. I used to try to talk like the girls here, to swing my hips when I walked, sneak menthols behind the bleachers and drink soda from crinkled cans. To feel something toward the football players who always seem to be getting cheerleaders like my mom pregnant. But the act inevitably fell flat. So now I try to stay relatively unknown, to not speak too loudly in class or do anything that could call attention to me and my secret.

I feel like a criminal, almost. Despite everything I do, I wonder if they still know when I pass them in the halls. Know about the desire that I sometimes think is slowly eating me alive. Or about Sarah and me. All that kissing. Or about me and Jean. This constant paranoia comes with being closeted in a town so small everyone spends too much time trying to find out everyone else's secrets just so they don't expire of boredom. It sounds crazy, but nothing's safe.

   I wonder what Rosie is thinking as she blows bubble after bubble.

 卐   卐   卐

AT ROSIE'S fifteenth birthday party, I slipped. Madonna had just kissed Britney on TV and the girls were all talking about it. Rosie couldn't keep the disgust out of her voice; her mouth got all screwed up just from thinking of the brief spectacle of that kiss, the silence that came over the crowd when their lips met. We were all in her living room, holding melting glasses of root beer floats, and she leaned in close to me, her mouth inches away from mine, and reflexively I closed my eyes.

Immediately I realized my mistake and jerked away from her, said in a voice that I knew wasn't convincing, "It's disgusting; they should be ashamed."

But it was too late and the other girls had all started squealing, "It looked like she was going to kiss her!"

Panicked, I started talking too fast about how I thought the new quarterback was dreamy, but the incident had left a sour aftertaste, a nagging feeling that just for a second, all those other girls had seen the real me, had seen the girl I had been hiding under layers of glittery blush, beneath long loose dresses with broken pieces of mirrors stitched into the skirt that, when you looked too long at them, reflected back a broken image of yourself: fragments making up the parts of a girl. But after that night, nobody ever mentioned it again.

▦ ▦ ▦

AFTER MY first class, the coffee is still burning in my throat, so I go to the bathroom to rinse out my mouth with the brownish water. When I look up, three girls are standing behind me. I've seen them at church and at different parties, but we've never spoken. I know they're on the cheerleading squad. I know that Lacey's cousin was one of the girls who disappeared after she was found with another girl at last year's prom. Now they're whispering, like the bathroom is a temple and I'm the offering. The tallest of the three steps forward.

"Raya, right?"

"Hi."

She smiles. "I'm Madison."

"I know."

Her nails are sharp, short points as they dig into my palms and I try not to wince. The second tallest steps forward. "I'm Sherry, and this is Lacey." She gestures at the smallest girl.

Lacey's braces are coated in bread and what looks like canned green beans. She's trying to get the food out of her mouth, but it's making it worse. She looks up, waves. "I like your dress."

"Thanks."

As I walk out of the bathroom, they whisper to each other. I catch only the word *queer*. With that word I feel a stab of fear in my stomach, wonder if the only reason they talked to me was because they know what I am too. But then I think maybe I'm just paranoid. Decide to forget about it.

▦ ▦ ▦

AT LUNCH I pull apart bits of my PB&J and pretend to be like the other girls with their bright glittery hungers. Like the carnivorous plants from *The Botany of the Natural World*, the only science book our school will assign because it's the only one that doesn't mention evolution. I wonder, sometimes, what it would be like to not have to hide your hunger, to be able to want like those girls do without having to conceal it, without having to practice walking, practice smiling.

Once I heard about other girls and older women like me. It was a late-night news broadcast: a woman maybe fifty years old, with short hair and a men's button-down, was talking into a microphone. She was telling the reporter about how her girlfriend had been in a car accident somewhere in

Mississippi, how the EMTs wouldn't let her into the ambulance with her, how, because of that, the woman she loved died alone. The reporter kept fiddling with her wedding ring, and when the woman started crying, she jerked the microphone away. She turned around and started to say something about the campaign for homosexual equality ramping up, but before I got to hear her finish, Grammy jumped up and turned the TV off, muttering about how repugnant it was while I stared at my lap and tried to maintain an expressionless calm.

Earlier this summer, before the kiss, I saw a commercial for a show called *The L Word.* Two women were kissing in a white room. One's shawl slipped off her shoulders and fell to the floor. Then the scene cut to another woman wearing men's clothes, her hair hanging jagged around her face. She was holding a pale, dark-haired girl in her arms. When they started kissing too, I cleared my throat and then changed the channel. I turned to Sarah, who was sitting next to me on the couch, and I saw something like recognition flit across her face. She said, under her breath, "Beautiful," and then, so lightly I almost didn't feel it, she touched my hand. We never talked about it or saw the commercial again. But it gave me a glimmer of hope that beyond Heterosexualandia, beyond Pieria and the straight, flat land of Texas, there was a place for girls like us.

Sarah might be a preacher's daughter, but when she's not in church, she's all James Dean. Wears her hair in a low bun, baggy men's pants, button-downs. She's got a little *Y*-shaped birthmark under her bottom lip, and she wears men's boots.

She sits down next to me, takes my hand under the table, and runs her fingers over the lines in my palm, which makes me shiver. But I glance up and see that Rosie's standing by our table and looking at me in a way that makes me realize she's on to us. I jerk my hand away from Sarah and slide down.

"Rosie's staring again," I whisper.

She nods, starts talking loudly about boys. Rosie walks away, doesn't look back at us, so I make the mistake of thinking we're safe and take her hand again.

The girls in this school have always reminded me of butterflies, with their bright clothes and their easy desires hatching out of them like wings. Already they're changing into creatures I will never morph into. In the afternoon light, Sarah looks different. When she turns to look at me, her eyes don't have their usual edge in them. I wonder if she could love a girl like me, and though I don't want to let it, I feel hope slowly working its way into my chest.

Back at Sarah's house after school, we make out until we hear her mother's car stalling in the driveway. She whispers, "Let's wait till tonight."

We eat dinner with her family. My hands are shaking. I'm afraid of what might happen tonight and afraid of what Rosie might do if she learns more, if she starts to suspect that our kiss wasn't really a joke.

Sarah's brother, John, also brought a friend tonight: Aristo. I've seen him around school, but he's never spent the night when I was here before. I wonder for a second if they're the same as Sarah and me. But I know from the easy way Aristo laughs at her daddy's jokes that they're not. Even though her house is as much my home as mine is, at these dinners I never let my hand linger over Sarah's for too long, make sure that my laugh isn't a little too bright. Though until now, I've never had a reason to need to be this careful around Sarah's parents.

That night Sarah tells her mom we're tired, going to sleep early.

She locks the door and pulls me into her, takes my clothes off slowly. Then we're naked in her bed, and while nothing that we do is unfamiliar, it feels like I've found a new world for the two of us, together in the dark.

▦   ▦   ▦

THE NEXT day we go back to her house, spend the night together. Then it's Saturday morning, and Grammy picks up a shipment of roses and gerbera daisies, and Sarah's parents are out grocery shopping, so we're in bed. I'm trying to go down on her for the first time under the blankets, but I'm not really sure what I'm supposed to be doing, so I just keep trying to spell out the alphabet with my tongue like I saw in a lezzie mag I found tucked into one of the reference books in the library, then spent the rest of the year trying to figure out who put it there.

In the picture, a woman with hair so crimson it looked like blood was on her knees, her head between the legs of a petite blonde. The blonde's mouth was open and her eyes were closed and I thought, at first, that she was being captured in the moment after screaming. Her lip gloss was smeared down her face, and she had bite marks on her thighs. I started to study the picture like it could explain everything that had pre-viously been unsaid, but then I saw one of the popular girls walking toward me, so I shoved the book back on the shelf. I thought about going back and looking for it, but I was too scared of being seen, worried it was some kind of trap. So I never did. And now I wish I had. While I'd hooked up with three girls since sleepaway camp in seventh grade, we never got past rubbing our bodies together in the dark, sometimes putting a leg between the other girl's. Once, Jean brushed her hands up my skirt and stopped a few inches before she reached my underwear. But other than that, our clothes always stayed on and we never acknowledged it the next day.

I'm starting to get the hang of it and Sarah's moving underneath me, gripping my hair and clenching her thighs around my head, when I hear something. Since no one's home, I think it's one of their cats running around, but then I hear laughter.

I sit up.

It's John's friend, Aristo. He doesn't say anything, just slams the bedroom door.

Sarah's eyes are wide and scared, and I feel dizzy. We get dressed shakily and run downstairs.

"It's not what you think," I blurt out. I pause after that, trying to come up with some sort of excuse even though I know it's futile, that it really is what he thinks, that I can't lie my way out of it.

He laughs. "What, you two were just playing doctor? You're a little old for that."

I'm opening my mouth to say something, though I don't know what.

I run after him barefoot and start to chase him down Sarah's driveway when he gets in the car with Sarah's brother. I rap on the glass, but when Aristo rolls down the window, I realize I can't beg him not to tell anyone in front of John, who's staring at me with a confused expression. So I just walk back to the house where Sarah's waiting on the porch.

I sit down next to her.

"Raya? What do we do now?"

"Maybe he won't tell anyone."

"You should probably go, just in case."

🔡 🔡 🔡

ON THE way home, I try to come up with excuses, but I know there's nothing I can do or say that will get me out of this. Back at the house, I keep waiting for the phone to ring, for Grammy to show up with the look of disappointment that I've gotten used to over the years, though this time her disappointment will be mixed with disgust. This time she'll look at me like she doesn't know me anymore, like she doesn't even want to, and there won't be anything I can do. I sit on the faded leather couch in the living room, trace the cracks in the seat where the coiled wires and pale bits of stuffing slip through, and wait for her to come back. Though I've been waiting for this to happen, have known for years that whatever I do to hide I'll still be found out, I'm terrified.

When I look at my hands, they're shaking, and my body doesn't feel like my own, as if I'm seeing myself from somewhere else far away.

The girl in question is small, awkward. Her cuticles are visibly ragged, scabs forming at the edge of her fingers from where she bites her nails. Her hair is wild, around her face in a frizzed-out cloud. When she stops mimicking the women she sees on TV, in magazines, and the girls at school, there's a subtle kind of sadness etched into her face. In the dying light, her makeup is smeared. Now that she's in the safety of her house, her shirt has slipped down and the scars on her back show, pale, almost knotted-looking lines where her wings were ripped out of her.

🏱 🏱 🏱

WHEN GRAMMY comes home, I watch her face for any sign of knowing. She just tosses me a plastic bag with a tub of vanilla Breyers and a chicken TV dinner in it. "I have to go out for a bit, but I brought you dinner." Before I can try to gauge what she knows and what she doesn't, she disappears upstairs.

She's gone long enough that the ice cream starts to melt, so I put it and the TV dinner in the freezer and go back to the couch, sit down carefully to avoid the sharp ridges of the split leather. When she comes downstairs, she's wearing red lipstick, and pale face powder is smudged over her cheeks. She's got on a black dress and the red pashmina I got her for her birthday last year.

"Grams?"

She smiles tearfully, smooths her dress with her hands. "How do I look?"

"You look beautiful."

"No, I don't."

"It's true."

Grammy sighs. "I haven't gone on a date since your grandfather. I was young then, so pretty all the boys would wait outside my house with flowers. But I wouldn't go out with any of them until I met your grandpa."

I don't respond. I never know what to say when she talks about my dead grandpa.

Grammy's quiet after that, probably because of all the time

she's spending with Paul. When Paul comes to pick her up, I'm as rude to him as I can be without outright snarling. I can't stand the thought of our already fragile balance being disrupted by an outsider, of having another person bear witness to our half-formed life together.

He hands me a daisy. I do my best to seem nonplussed, though I can't help but smile a little bit.

When they leave, I am unable to shake the feeling that I've been found out. I need to be ready for whatever happens next, so I sprint upstairs to fill my backpack with all the essentials in case I need to make a run for it: some clean clothes, a ten-dollar bill, a knife I got at a history museum a few years ago, and a plastic Ziploc with the picture of me and Mom. That's all I have that feels worth bringing with me if I have to go. I don't know how these things could save me, but it makes me feel better to have them ready.

⊞ ⊞ ⊞

ON SUNDAY Sarah's mom comes to pick me up. Since no one is acting strangely toward me, I begin to let myself think that maybe we're safe. When we go to her house for the night, I leave the backpack behind. Once her parents are asleep and the sounds of her house creaking and the night air are the only things around us, I kiss her for the first time since we were found, and my heart finally stops thudding and I sleep well.

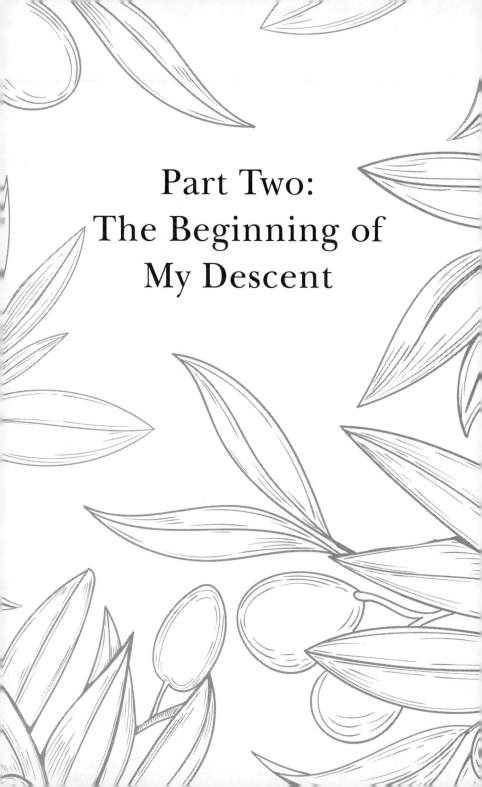

Part Two:
The Beginning of
My Descent

Monday at school the three girls from the bathroom are waiting for me at my locker. Madison steps forward. "There's a party tonight at Lacey's house. You and your friend should come." She gestures at Sarah, down the hall, back turned on us as she tries to open her locker. "It starts at eight."

"Okay."

She hands me a paper with the address scrawled on it.

When they're gone, Sarah ambles up. "What did they want?"

"They invited us to a party tonight at Lacey's house. What do you think?" I try to make my voice sound neutral.

I've been to only one school party in the past year, after a football game. Everyone drank spiked punch in the bleachers once the parents went home, and the cheerleaders kicked their shoes off and danced in circles around the field. I watched from a distance, afraid that if I drank I'd let myself go, even for a second, and then somehow I'd slip and they'd all know. So like always, I just sat on the edge of the field and watched everyone, taking mental notes about what they were all doing, gestures and phrases that I could mirror later when I pretended to be like them.

After, I walked back from the party and stood in front of the bathroom mirror with the door locked. I piled my hair into one of the high, tight ponytails the girls at school wore. I'd watch them roam the halls like strange ibis birds, bobbing through the sea of high schoolers. The ponytail required that you comb your hair flat to your head, then twist the ponytail elastic so tight it would give you a migraine. Crimp the ends so that they fanned out of your head like feathers. When you took the elastic out, hair would be wrapped around the tie. Sometimes I'd yank the hair out on purpose just to marvel at the neatness with which something could come away from my body, then stare at the dark strands nestled in my palms. I'd always feel a sharp regret, the kind that comes with seeing something you wanted to destroy and also to save be ruined.

I'd tried repeating some of the things I'd heard girls say to their boyfriends. I'd said the names of every boy on the football team. I'd swirled the shimmering hot pink blush that I'd bought before school started onto my cheeks, but it just made me look fevered and more desperate. So I'd washed the blush off quickly, jerking the washcloth over my cheeks so roughly that it left my skin redder than it had been before. And then, quietly so Grammy wouldn't hear, I cried for a long, long time.

Now, Sarah twists her hair around her fingers. "We should go. I don't think anybody knows. It'd be fun."

For a second I wonder if this is a bad idea, if we should stay home. But she smiles at me, her eyes bright with excitement, and I decide not to worry so much.

🔡 🔡 🔡

AFTER SCHOOL we go back to her house and sit nervously through dinner with her parents, then tell them we're going to work on a group project at a friend's. We walk the three miles to the party, holding hands in the dark. Before we turn into the neighborhood, she pulls me into the part of the road that's hidden by trees and kisses me.

When we get to the house, the yard is thrumming with teen bodies. Drunk girls are draping themselves over the porch railing. A boy's throwing up in the front lawn. The musky scents of Drakkar Noir and Juicy Couture, sweat and beer fills the air. It's one of those nights where the dark emptiness of the sky stretches out before you, huge and unmoored in its possibility.

For a minute I think that anything is possible. That I could kiss Sarah right here, face the consequences of whatever will happen in the morning. But then she's pulling on my arm, so I step inside.

Aristo is there, in the front room. He's drunk already, slurring.

He lopes over to us, wraps his arms around our shoulders. "My girls."

I try to push his arm off me but he pulls me in tighter,

so tight that when he lets go, I know I'll have white finger-prints on my upper arm. I notice that people are starting to watch. Rosie, resplendent in a fuchsia sequined halter top and a tangerine-orange silk skirt with a camo jacket and high-heeled platform sandals that she can't seem to balance in, stares intently with an expression that flutters between disgust and desire.

Aristo tries to kiss my cheek but I duck. He lets go of both of us and I start to run away, but he grabs my arm, pulls me closer. Says in a low voice, "The way I see it, you kind of owe me for not telling anyone that you're bull-dyking out together."

Then he tries to kiss me, but this time I punch him hard enough that his nose starts bleeding. He pushes me and I fall down.

I realize now that we never should have come to this party.

The room goes so quiet I don't think anyone is breathing. He doesn't say anything, just covers his hand with the sleeve of his shirt and tries to wipe away the blood with it.

Sarah steps forward, her voice low and scary when she says, "Leave her alone."

He turns, and for a minute I think he's going to leave, that what I have a feeling is about to happen isn't going to happen.

But instead of leaving, he goes out to the back porch. He throws his arms up, yells, "Everyone, I have an announce-ment to make." He seems drunker than he did a few minutes ago, keeps swaying. I try to will my body to get up, to go stop him, but I can't move. I'm trapped. And it's like in the dream with the wings: everyone's staring at me and I have the feeling that I'm about to be changed, that something is going to come exploding out of me, and with it will come the truth.

"These two"—Aristo points at me and Sarah—"they're lesbos." He's screaming. "I saw them carpet-munching each other. Disgusting."

Then, just like in my dream, everyone turns and stares at me, and I know that nothing will be the same again.

Sarah lets go of the neck of the bottle that she was holding and it shatters on the floor. "That's not true. He's just mad because she wouldn't let him kiss her."

But I know that they have already decided what the truth is.

Everyone is staring at us, a mixture of anger and revulsion mottling their faces, their expressions ugly. One boy raises a beer bottle and gestures like he's going to throw it at us. Rosie has turned to another girl, and they're whispering loudly about how they knew something was wrong with me, with Sarah.

We bolt, start running once we reach the end of Lacey's driveway.

I look back only once, see that everyone, including Sarah's brother, watches to see where we are going. Lacey and Madison are following us, but stop at the edge of Lacey's lawn and watch us leave.

🂠 🂠 🂠

THAT NIGHT Sarah's brother John doesn't come home from the party, and neither does Aristo. We stay up all night watching for headlights, but none come. Eventually, when the sun starts to rise, we fall asleep for an hour before we have to get up for school. I dress care-fully, swirl on blush and cake on eyeshadow, rim my eyes with teal-blue liner. I wear one of Sarah's pink church dresses, even though it's too late, I've already been found.

When I get to my locker, there are several papers taped to it. They all say DYKE or FAG. I peel them off the metal like scabs, crumple them up and put them in my backpack. It should be a surprise, but I've known this moment would come for so long, and now that it's happening, it feels like another one of my nightmares.

When I look up, Rosie is glaring at me. She mouths, "Fag."

I think about smiling at her, pretending it's nothing, but instead something sharp lodges itself under my rib cage and I move forward. I've decided if I'm going to come out, I'm going to come out swinging. I square my shoulders. My body is like a car on black ice spinning out in the road, something that's beyond my control now.

"Fuck you—I'm a dyke."

It comes out fast and hard, and when she opens her mouth, I know that I might as well have gone and put a gun between my lips and pulled the trigger. Just like that, it's all over, and I know that it's the end of my life as I knew it.

I regret it instantly. I know that now, after spending so many years obsessing over staying invisible, for the first time I'm being seen, and not in the way I wanted to be. The event that I've been dreaming about for so many years has finally taken place, and I can't go back or wake up and pray with Grammy.

Can't lie and say that I dreamed about Mom or Jesus again, though I never did know why I felt like I had to cover up the dream about my wings.

Now it's happening. After all those wasted nights when I couldn't sleep, nights when I stayed awake thinking of what would happen. Running through my head all of the things I could have done to better hide myself. Remembering all of the times I'd slipped up and looked at a girl for too long and then seen someone else looking at my looking. Flushing a deep red, awkwardly mumbling something about liking the girl's dress, even though it wasn't the dress that was turning my face hot and making me clench and unclench my hands into fists until my knuckles turned white.

I'm moving. It feels like I'm underwater, my legs trembling, I walk away from Rosie, who's shaking with something akin to anger. I'm not worried about them knowing that I'm gay. I'm just worried about what Grammy will do to me, what Sarah's parents will do to her. Mostly I worry about what the other kids and the town will do. If they'll make me disappear, or worse. The crowd disperses when I reach the door leading out of the cafeteria, and soon only one boy remains watching.

Once I knew a boy from church who got found. Later I heard that the boy's father saw him kissing another boy and tried to exorcise the gay out of them. Beat them with a cane and prayed in tongues until they swore they were cured. Nobody saw either boy again. Their parents sent them away. To be cured by one of the conversion facilities Texas is so proud of, or to be forgotten like yesterday's sermon: reduced to the memory of a few words and some stray images you can't place. Two boys. Gone completely. That's what happens to gay teens in this town. They get disappeared.

Or it's like what happened with the girls they found last year, girls who never returned. They too got turned into cautionary tales about what happens to queers around here.

When I first heard about the girls and the boys, I was scared but unsurprised. I had always known that one day one of us would be caught, and that one day, as long as I lived here, I too would be found, like in the dream when my wings come bursting out of my back. I knew I would change in their eyes and morph into something beyond anyone's ability to love. That I would be changed into something Grammy could never find beautiful.

I walk to my last class of the day, try to ignore everyone staring at me and the steady panic that's rising in my throat and leaving a burning taste on my tongue. Sarah's nowhere to be found. I convince myself that she just changed her mind about coming to school today. But something feels wrong. I have a feeling that something has happened to her. I think about last night, how when we were crouched in the dark of her bedroom looking out the window, waiting for John to come home and to tell her parents the secret that was no longer one, she had turned to me— and though she didn't say anything, she didn't have to. In her room with only the moon for light, it was dim enough that all I could see were her eyes, but her eyes were all I needed to see to know that in that moment, she was on the brink of falling in love with me. To know that she was young and beautiful and lost and close to being mine. And

I knew that I had passed the verge of having fallen and had already plummeted, that I was already hers, that I would do anything for her.

⊞ ⊞ ⊞

AFTER SCHOOL Grammy comes to pick me up, which is something she almost never does. I can't tell what she knows, if she knows, though when she looks at me, disappointment is etched into her face. Her hands shake as she opens the Volvo's door. She clenches the steering wheel as she drives. I take a deep breath, waiting for the ax to fall.

"Grammy, is something wrong?"

"Paul wants me to marry him."

Relief that she doesn't know yet makes it easier for me to breathe again. I suck in my breath, try to imagine what life would be like with another person intruding on our solitude, but right now that's the least of my worries.

"That's amazing. What did you say?"

"I said I don't know." But she smiles more brightly than I've ever seen her smile before. Grammy finally looks over at me. "After service, want to skip the banquet and you and me can go get some pie, maybe see a movie?"

"Sure, I'd like that." I try to wipe the worry off my face. To smile sincerely.

Grammy grins, sings along with the muted gospel music leaking out of the radio. When she gets to the part where the chorus starts up, I try to join her. "When God calls me by his side, on angel's wings I'll arrive," but my voice cracks and my eyes start to sting from suppressed tears. I turn to the window and watch the familiar landscape blur, and try to keep the sadness from flooding over me. But she doesn't notice, just keeps singing until the radio cuts into a soft, low buzz of static—and still smiling, she switches it off and lets a heavy silence fill the car.

While Grammy's napping, I go upstairs to Mom's room and let myself in quietly.

I never go to her room when Grammy's home, but today I know it's the only thing that can begin to calm me down. I lie down on the bed she once slept in and stare at the water stain on the corner of the ceiling. The stain keeps spreading. One day it will engulf the ceiling completely. When it does, we won't be able to keep Mom's room exactly the way she left it anymore, and we will have to decide whether to mend the ceiling for the room that neither of us uses or to cover the furniture in plastic so the mold doesn't get to it.

Either way, I'll lose her.

※ ※ ※

BEFORE CHURCH I change into a pale pink dress and tie my hair into a braid with a long sky-blue satin ribbon. I wash the makeup off my face, dab the perfume and scented lotion that Grammy buys me onto my skin. I know it's too late for this disguise, that I've already been found out, but I can't help trying. I've been invisible for so long that I don't know how to be seen after having spent so much of my life trying to pass unnoticed. For so many years, I've spent every day trying to decide what to wear to hide who I am, spent so much time buying makeup and shoes and hair dye, thinking that it could mask my gayness—thinking that if I assimilated enough and dyed enough blonde chunks into my bangs then I could stay unseen, that it would keep me safe, camouflage me. But I never let myself truly believe the life I'd started was nothing more than a prelude to its loss.

In the car I try to push my growing panic back down, to slow my breath. It's only when I look at my lap that I realize I'm gripping my Bible so tightly that my hands have turned red from the pressure. When I get out of the car, my legs are shaking but I manage to still them enough to walk. Once inside the church, I collapse into the first chair I see. Sarah's father is watching me with a strained expression. Sarah's mom won't look at me, stares straight ahead at the pews. I know they know. I have the sudden urge to start running but realize it would only make things worse.

Grammy waves at them, sits down next to me. My heart is thudding so hard and fast in my chest that I think I'm going to get sick.

"Grammy? I don't feel good. We should go."

She ignores me, stands up and goes over to hug Sarah's mom. And Sarah's mom, when she sees Grammy coming her way, looks at me, and when she looks at me, I know that it's all over. There's no escaping what's going to happen. I know that Sarah and I will disappear. The ax has fallen. I close my eyes, squeeze them shut so tightly it hurts, and I don't open them again until Grammy comes back to sit next to me. She's pale and her lips are set into a thin line. Her voice, when she turns to me, is shaking. "I don't feel well either. Let's go."

I know that I should say something, that I should lie, but what can I say? After all these years of waiting to be found out, even before I knew I was gay, before I knew what my secret was, what it meant, I've known that one day Grammy would look at me like this, with a combination of disgust and terrible sadness spreading across her face, making her features broken. And so I say nothing, hope that if I don't say anything, then what I know is coming won't happen.

"Okay. Just let me run to the bathroom." I understand now that I won't be seeing Sarah anytime soon. I want to try to find her before what happened to those girls happens to me.

"You can wait until we get home," Grammy says.

I walk quietly behind her, feel everyone's eyes burning into my back as I leave.

Outside the church, Lacey is waiting. I haven't seen her since she stood at the edge of her yard and watched us go. She comes running up to me, breathless.

"Sarah got sent away. To anti-homo camp. To get fixed."

Grammy grabs my arm and squeezes hard enough to leave fingerprints. "We need to go now, Raya."

I wrench my arm out of Grammy's grasp. "What do you mean?" I ask Lacey.

She balances on one leg, snaps her gum. "I'm really sorry, Raya." Then she sees Madison and runs to her.

I'm alone. Sarah's gone. I wonder what those girls felt the night they were found with their arms around each other. For a second were they relieved, just a little bit, that they didn't have to live with their secret anymore?

⊞ ⊞ ⊞

GRAMMY AND I drive back to the house in silence. We're nearing the daisy field when Grammy pulls over onto the side of the road. She puts her blue-gray head down on the steering wheel. I try to put my hand on her shoulder but she slaps it away, chokes out, "Don't touch me." The way she says it, it's more of a cry of disgust than a demand. And that hurts me more than anything else she could have said.

Once we're home, she doesn't speak to me, and I know that no matter what happens, it's over. The relationship that neither of us ever really wanted to have in the first place is gone. I sit at the kitchen table and stay there, even after she goes upstairs and I hear her door close. I sit there a long time, just watching the light above the stove flicker like the fireflies Sarah and I used to catch on balmy summer nights. We'd sit on her porch, our knees touching, cupping our hands together, heads brushing against each other. We could spend hours watching them glow in the warm dark while the cicadas shrilled around us. It's then that I start to cry, not for myself, but for the two girls who are gone.

I first knew that I would love her when we were twelve. She woke me up at three in the morning just so she could show me the North Star outside of her window. Without saying anything, she took my hand and didn't let go until the sun was rising and the star was gone. We never talked about it again.

🔲 🔲 🔲

AT SOME point I must have fallen asleep because Grammy is standing next to me, telling me to get up. And while her voice isn't kind, it isn't not, so at first I think it was all a dream, but then I see that she's packed all of my things into four paper bags. The morning light is harsh, and I can feel the beginnings of a headache.

"Grammy?"

"We need to leave."

"Why?"

She sighs. "I'm sorry, Raya, but I just can't raise a queer. It's not natural. You were"—her voice catches—"you were supposed to be my second chance. Lord knows I deserved one. I need to do it right this time. And you're just not right. You're sick. It's a sickness, really. I don't know how I let it go on so long. I just didn't want to believe it, all the stories about you. I just can't let you live like this. So I'm taking you to get better. It's a good place; Preacher Sam recommended it. It's run through his pastor friend's church. The pastor's son is in charge. He sent Sarah there too. We need to get going."

But I've stopped listening. *Sarah.*

⊞ ⊞ ⊞

I BRUSH my teeth with my finger and try to pull back my hair into a high bun, but the elastic snaps. I give up trying to look presentable, let my hair fall in a bird's nest around my face. I sneak upstairs and grab the backpack with my emergency supplies, then I shove it into a paper bag along with the rest when she isn't looking.

Alone, looking into the trunk of the car, I realize that my whole life can fit in four paper bags, which don't even take up the entire trunk. I can feel something sharp wedging its way into my throat. I think about running as fast as I can, about not saving Sarah but just saving myself. I could get a job working nights at a fast-food place, live in a run-down motel room until I could look for her and could try to save her, though it would probably be too late.

Grammy emerges from the house with two mugs of coffee, and I climb into the front seat and just give in to the uncertainty of everything. The Volvo, by some terrible miracle, starts on the first try, something that has not happened for as long as I can remember, and I look back at the house of my girlhood, and even after we're far away, I still look back. From now on, a girl isn't something I'll have the luxury of being, and as I watch Pieria disappear from my line of sight, I feel the beginning of an abrupt ending to what was left of my childhood, and I start to cry again.

⊞ ⊞ ⊞

WE DRIVE for hours. We stop only to get gas and a bottle of soda pop, the orange-flavored kind. The woman behind the register at the station is wearing dream catcher earrings and a long, pale green prairie dress. She smiles at me sympathetically when she sees Grammy's expression, and for a minute I entertain another fantasy of begging this elderly woman to save me, even though I know she can't. I leave the Fanta on the back seat, and by the time I drink it, the carbonation has gone flat.

The landscape changes from the flat green of Pieria to barren fields. This part of Texas is populated with washed-out trees, their leaves barely hanging on to the branches. Though it's early fall, the air is cold. I shiver, try not to think about what's going to happen to me, just replay my last night with Sarah in my mind. Remember how she was in my arms, it felt like we were becoming something other than girls who had spent their whole lives running from themselves.

Eventually we pull onto a private road. There's a sign that

reads FRIENDLY SAVIORS, and I know that I'm being disappeared. It's then I decide that I'm going to descend into the
depths of the underworld just like Orpheus, and I'm going
to save the girl I love. Because Orpheus? She's a girl, who
likes girls.

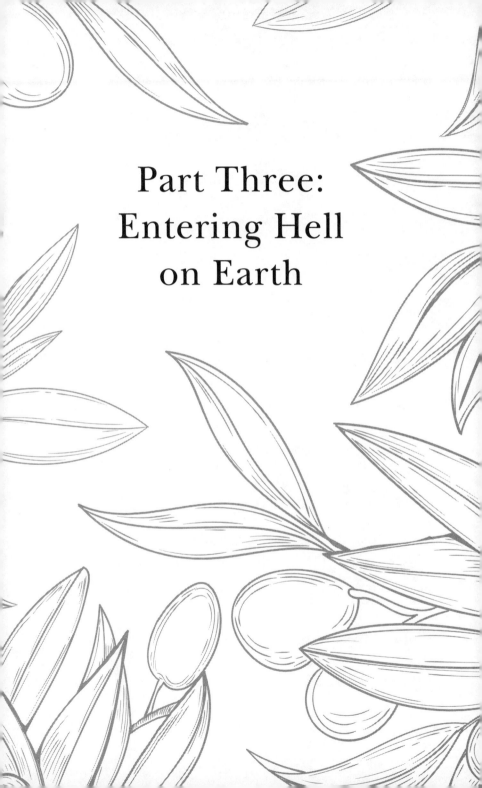

Part Three:
Entering Hell
on Earth

I step out of the car with my head held high. The driveway leading up to the camp is muddy, and dirt sticks to my shoes, spatters my legs. This is the middle of nowhere. The only neighbors we'll have are trees and the wide stretch of sky that hangs low and blue over the horizon like a bride's drooping veil.

Now that the thing I've spent so many years avoiding is happening, I mostly feel numb. All I want is to see Sarah. So I try to think only about her on the night we walked home from the party, how she held me close and the moonlight cast shadows on her skin. She told me she loved me then, and I didn't answer. I think she thought it was because I didn't love her back, but really, I just loved her too much, so much that I couldn't speak. I was too overwhelmed by everything.

A pale man wearing faded, baggy clothes is waiting for me at the entrance. To the left side of the house, there's a stretch of forest flanked by tall pine trees. The house has three stories and a little driveway on the side with a scratched red pickup truck parked in it. A small garden is in front with nothing but a few straggly tomatoes and what looks like a lavender bush that has been overrun by weeds. Upon closer inspection, I realize there's a second, smaller house at the other end of the property. No lights are on and it looks slightly abandoned. The glass in the porch light's busted, and the wooden porch is covered in a slippery-looking moss.

The bigger house is gray, and I tell myself it almost looks like a boarding school, but really it looks like a prison. I can see what I think is a football field filled with large rocks behind the house. There's an orange cat on the front porch with a strange dent in its tail and a lazy, clouded-over eye. That's all I can see from the driveway. I think I see a face appear briefly in one of the windows, but when I watch the windows for any sign of life, the face doesn't come back. The man who greeted me holds out his hands and, before I can react, grabs both of mine and peers uncomfortably intensely into my eyes. His eyes are so blue they remind me of a jellyfish—they have the same transparent quality—and his blond hair is buzzed so short that I can see his pink scalp.

"I'm Hyde. I run the program. I'll be helping you get back on your path to Jesus." He smiles, and I notice he's missing a front tooth. He sees me looking at it. "That was from before I found God."

Before I can reply, a tall, icy blonde woman comes out

onto the porch. She's wearing a doctor's lab coat over tan riding pants.

She holds a hand out coolly. "My name's Char. I'm the doctor."

It's unclear whether I'm supposed to shake or kiss her hand, so I do neither and just stand there awkwardly. Grammy's worrying her cross necklace, her forehead crinkled up. Suddenly I want to shake her, to beg her not to leave me here, but I know it wouldn't do anything. She's already made up her mind.

Then a petite girl wearing a "Jesus ROCKS!" T-shirt comes out. "Raya, right? My name's Clio. Let's get you settled in." She's wearing a long, shapeless, purple corduroy overall dress underneath the T-shirt, and her twists are wrapped up in a bright yellow headband.

I turn to her. "What are you here for?"

She grins sadly. "I fell in love at a bad time."

Under my breath I say, "Me too," but quietly, so she won't hear me.

Before she opens the front door and ushers me into the house, she puts a hand on my shoulder, smiles at me, and for a second I feel hopeful.

Then, just like that, she's gone.

⌗ ⌗ ⌗

INSIDE THE house I give my name, height, and weight to a boy. He's washed out and nervous-seeming. He looks like a sick elf. He's got bandages wrapped around his wrists. His legs rock back and forth, kicking the desk. His brown hair has been buzzed—almost bald like the man I met outside.

His hands tremble so much that while he's typing things I can't see into the computer, he brings one hand up to the other to still the shaking.

My stomach drops a little bit when I see what looks like red suction marks on the inside of his wrist, as if something tried to suck the queerness out of him.

Eventually he finishes typing and looks up from the computer.

"My name's Jason. You're all entered in. I think this program will be good for you, Raya. It will help. It helped me. I used to be despicable"—his voice cracks in a way that sounds like a sob—"changed by Satan into something that even Jesus couldn't love. And now I'm seeing a nice girl here, Clio. We're going to get married as soon as we both complete the program. I can go back to trying to become a pastor like my dad was. I was going to be one, you know. Before everything."

I don't respond. I've forced myself to go to that strange, calm place that girls can access only when they're in trouble. The kind where you leave your body like you're already dead, ball your fists until your fingers turn white, and pretend to be anywhere else but where you are right now. You take a deep breath but don't exhale, just wait for the violence you know is coming for you. I learned how to do this in kindergarten when boys would throw rocks at me because I didn't have parents, because I told our teacher I didn't want a husband, only a pet horse. Even then I knew what I was, though I wasn't smart enough to hide.

When I learned, finally, that I was gay, I realized I'd always been hiding, but all those years before, I just didn't know what I was hiding from, why my heart was always racing, why

I always felt like I was only mimicking going through the motions of my girlhood.

Whenever their rocks hit the back of my head, I'd close my eyes until the dull ache had faded to nothing but the memory of pain. I try to do that now, to forget what's happening until after it already has.

When Jason is done registering me, he hands me a plastic clip-on name tag and I snap back to reality.

Grammy comes inside and signs some papers. She's still crying. Tears fall from her face and smudge her signature.

"I'm sorry. Okay. I'll call you every time I get the chance."

Then she's gone too.

卍   卍   卍

AFTER GRAMMY leaves, the panic sets in. My backpack with the knife and my journals are now with Hyde for "safe-keeping." I realize now that everything I grew up with, everything I've ever known, is gone. Before this, I've never been farther than twenty miles from Pieria. The only time I've left was in eighth grade, when my class went to the aquarium. I remember pressing my hands against the wall made out of glass, watching the strange aquatic creatures bob around, and though I didn't know why, I cried.

Jason makes me empty my pockets. All I have is a pen, a candy bar, and a photo of Sarah and me that I tucked into my waistband. He takes everything except for the picture, which remains hidden.

In it Sarah had just turned fourteen, and we're celebrating

by going out to dinner with her parents. We're both wearing dresses. The light in the photo obscures my face so you can see only a shadow in the shape of a girl, and Sarah's smiling, illuminated. For once, one of the dresses her parents always wanted her to wear seems natural. She looks like she could have been someone else, but also happy in a way that was rare for her. That's why I kept the photo next to my bed, why I brought it with me. Back in Pieria, on nights we weren't together, I'd look at it, imagine that maybe we really were the girls that we looked like in that picture.

I realize that a small crowd is gathering around me. A couple of girls and a boy. One of the girls is wearing a T-shirt: "ACCEPT THE SAVIOR INTO YOUR HEART, AND NEVER WANT AGAIN!" It's then I decide that I'm going to be the biggest, baddest lesbian these hateful freaks have ever seen.

Hyde leads me to a bathroom and gives me a pile of clothes. There is a faded denim skirt. It is ankle-length, too big around the waist. I have to hold it up with a belt. Hyde helps me punch an extra hole with a pocketknife so it won't fall back down. They let me keep my red sneakers and my black lace bra. But they make me put on weird granny-style cotton under-wear and a T-shirt with a Jesus slogan on it. Mine reads "JESUS SAVED ME! HE CAN SAVE YOU TOO!" It's only when Hyde leads me outside into the backyard that I realize that everyone here is wearing a Jesus T-shirt. I keep looking around anxiously. I'm starting to worry that Sarah's not here, that she's at a different camp. I think about calling out for her, but I am afraid of giving anything away. There are about eight of us.

Then I see her.

It's like I'm not really seeing her, because the person I'm looking at is no longer Sarah, just some broken shell that resembles her. She's wearing a dress that somehow makes her look even gayer and she's shaking with cold, though it's a warm evening, balmy even. She has a blank look on her face, like she's no longer there.

Even though I know we'll both pay for it, I run to her. My heart is beating too fast, and I think maybe they got to her, did to her whatever they did to those other girls.

"Sarah?"

She looks at me. Her long hair is gone, cropped close to her head in raggedy patches, like grass that's been poorly mowed. Her eyes seem washed out. She's dressed the same as me, but they made her put a silky pink bow in her short hair. Without the makeup her mother used to foist on her, and despite the bow and the dress, with her shaved head she almost looks like the girl she always wanted to be.

I can feel a sob rising in my throat at what they've done to her. Her eyes look vacant, like pictures I saw of towns after they've been bombed: empty craters, shadows shaped like their old residents. She's looking behind me—at Hyde. He watches us with his head cocked for a minute then shakes it, like he's forgotten something, and goes inside. When he's gone, her eyes regain their normal sparkle and she winks at me.

"Sorry for freaking you out," she whispers. "I just have to act like I've been lobotomized. Or else they make me sit by myself in this room and talk to this freaky woman, Char, who's kind of not there—like, mentally—at all. I think she's an actual serial killer, I swear. God, it's good to see you. I heard them talking last night, heard them say your name, how Grammy found out, needed to get you fixed. They didn't mention me, though, so I don't think they know about us yet."

She takes a red apple out of her pocket. In the colorless yard, where the sky is faded and even the people look bleached, the brightness of the apple makes it look precious. She tosses it to me and I bite into it.

It's so sweet it makes me gag. I think maybe we can get out of here, and when I watch Sarah, her eyes glitter with something akin to hope.

As I take in Sarah's hair with its ridiculous baby bow, I decide that the first thing I'm doing tonight is shaving my head. Let's see them try to straighten up that. I start laughing at the idea of my bald head with little pink bows affixed to it. Maybe a tiny pink baby bonnet.

Sarah's face crumples.

"What?" I whisper.

"It's my fault. I'm really sorry."

Hyde calls for us to come back inside. He says we're doing a prayer circle. The room has green walls and no furniture except for thirteen plastic fold-up chairs arranged in a circle, with Hyde, Jason, and Char in the center. Char, I notice, has a hungry, almost wolfish look about her.

I can feel my heart thudding somewhere in my chest. I've heard the stories about what they do to you here.

Hyde explains to me that in these circles everyone has to go around and say why we're here. We must describe our sins and then say what we want to be, who we want to become once we leave the program cured of our unnatural desires.

Diane, a blonde girl with the shoulders of a football quarterback and a kind of butch swagger that even the hyperfeminine outfits all the girls are wearing can't change, goes first.

"Well, my sin—I mean, where I went wrong—it was definitely when I was going to school, you know, and I played football on the boys' team"—I was right!—"and there was this girl, Mary."

"Go on," Hyde says, even though he's staring at me.

"And, well, one night after the game we were showering together because I had to use the cheerleaders' locker room to clean up and not the boys' one, which really didn't help me, and Mary, she was so pretty, and I guess she kind of just got in the shower with me . . ." Here, she trails off.

"And that was when you sinned?" Hyde asks.

"We sinned and then another girl found us and told."

"And you know now that what you were doing was an affront against Jesus Christ himself? And now that you're here with us, you're ready to accept him into your heart and cast aside the homosexual desire that Satan has spawned in you?"

"Yes."

The boy next to me—a beautiful, flamboyant boy with a Russian accent and blue-black curls—seems to be the one patient I've seen who's as outwardly gay and unrepentant as I am. He nudges me and whispers, "Actually, it was the whole cheerleading squad, not some girl named Mary. Their coach found them."

When Hyde cuts us a look, the boy makes the blow-job face until Hyde flushes a deep crimson.

The boy's name is Leon. Later I learn that he's an army brat who spent his childhood trekking around Russia. Before he moved to Mississippi and got sent here, to a facility so deep in the middle of Texas that his father hoped nobody from their new town would find out, he lived in Moscow. His mother had died suddenly from an illness that was diagnosed after it was too late to save her, and his father took a job in America. Finding himself facing the pressures of the Deep South, pressures that in some ways were worse than in Moscow, he shipped Leon off. From what Leon says, it sounds like his father doesn't actually hate his son's gayness. He just wants to make his son's life easier in some misguided but well-meaning way.

The group keeps going around. There is a "girl" who is really a boy, and whenever he speaks Hyde snaps, "In your natural voice, not so deep," and he has to raise his voice to an unnaturally shrill tone. He is the only one they've made wear a full-on dress. It is an atrocity, hot pink and frilly, bunching awkwardly around the shoulders.

Hyde and Char call him Maia, but I make a note to call him Michael—his real name—when they aren't around.

Today his confession is that he stared at himself in the mirror, stared at the body they'd turned into something not his own, and started to cry. "Like a girl," Hyde says. "Good."

There is a girl named Karma who is here because her father found her with their maid's daughter. He disowned her, saying he'd rather let all his money go to waste than pass it on to a homosexual. When she learned he had cancer, she agreed to come here. Maybe her presence is all part of some elaborate plot to fake being converted to heterosexuality until the old guy blitzes, then go back to lezzing it up. That's what I hope, anyway; otherwise it's just too sad.

Karma sounds perpetually stoned, like Jean always did.

Listening to her reminds me of home and Jean's thick honeyed voice, how her throat was always gravelly with smoke, and also of the other girls at my school who would come in on Monday mornings with that same glazed look, the raspy aftermath from the night before still edged into their sleepy voices.

After Karma speaks, Hyde says, "Everyone, this is Karma's last night. Give her a round of applause." I think I see a tear fall down Karma's face. Everyone starts clapping wildly, so I join in.

Hyde stands up, puts a hand on her shoulder. "Karma fought her demons, and she won. She overcame them and found the light in a remarkably short amount of time. She's truly blessed to have walked through the fires of damnation and to have come out saved." He smiles down at her. "She's one of our greatest successes."

Karma's cheeks are red. Her bottom lip trembles with what I think is anger, but after a second she collects herself and says, "Thank you." She sounds like she means it. Jason stares at her with something like jealousy marring his face.

There are only ten of us—counting staff—in the room, and when Clio notices me looking around quizzically, she leans in and stage-whispers, "Sometimes if we're good, we get to skip the last session of the day."

At that moment Hyde turns to me. "Raya? Why don't you share your story of how you strayed from the path of Jesus Christ and became a sinner?"

I stay quiet. My heart is beating so quickly that for a second I think maybe they can hear it.

"Raya, if we're to cure you of this disease, you need to share with us how you got here."

I take a deep breath, don't look at Sarah, because if she looks at me, I know I'd choose the path of least resistance and pretend to be cured instantaneously just so I can be with her. And that I cannot do. To protect myself I've already created an entire fake life history—a persona to act out—because if I'm pretending to be someone else, they won't be able to get to me. I tell myself that they can't break a girl who doesn't exist because all they'll be breaking is a figment of my imagination.

I clear my throat and try to talk in the toughest voice I can manage. "Well, like the rest of you, I sinned as much as I could. Actually, they called me the lesbian Don Juan in my town."

Sarah sniffs, a laugh. When Hyde turns to her, she fakes a deep, hacking cough.

I forge on. "Yeah, I guess the homecoming queen's boyfriend got mad and told someone who then told everyone. He was probably upset his girlfriend dumped him for me."

Slowly Leon starts to clap. Hyde shushes him. He starts clapping again. Hyde shushes him again. It goes on like this for a few minutes. Then Hyde and Char turn to me. When I see the expressions on their faces, my stomach sinks.

Char's eyes burn into mine, and she says that I'm "a sinner, disgusting, unholy," that I "need to learn the error of my ways."

I feel my face go hot with shame. I don't know what to do, so I just mumble, "I'm fine."

It's a bad idea because over the pulsing blood in my ears, I can hear Hyde saying that I am going to rot in hell, be consumed in brimstone and fire with all the other sinners, and that I'll still be cold. It's frightening, and even though I don't believe in any of it, I start to get a little queasy. I don't respond. Hyde, now finished with his speech, is staring at me expectantly. I gaze at my lap.

Char clears her throat. "Raya? You need to acknowledge that what you've done is wrong if you want to heal. You need to repent."

I look up and see Sarah, who's watching me nervously, fidgeting.

So I take a deep breath and say, "I'm sorry, I guess."

Char smiles, doesn't say anything. Hyde nods approvingly.

During all of this, I maintain the stubborn grin of a girl who cares about nothing. The truth is I'm terrified. But over the years I've learned how to retreat inside of myself, how to kill the girl inside me and reinvent myself again and again and again, to lie so much I start to believe it. So that's what I've decided to do.

Sarah's next. She sits up straighter. "I fell in love with a girl." She looks up at the ceiling, won't make eye contact. My mouth is dry, cottony. Then she looks at me. "She was my best friend, but I loved her. Then my brother's friend saw us, and that was it." She crosses her arms over her chest, juts out her chin, almost as if she's daring them to challenge her.

Char says, "But you know that's wrong, right? That you committed a sin?"

Sarah's arms fall to her sides, and she looks sadder than I've ever seen her, sad in a way that makes my stomach hurt.

🔠 🔠 🔠

AFTER THE group ends, Hyde brings me to the rec room. It has three couches, a bookshelf, a pool table, a table with a pile of board games, and one half-dead TV that's airing only static. A few minutes later he returns with my backpack.

"Sorry, it's against rules for you to keep the knife and journals, but everything else is okay. I'll show you your room."

He leads me into a hallway that opens into a series of rooms. I see Leon disappear into one at the far end. They're all the same. The doors are all open. It reminds me of sleepaway camp: each room is small and spare and composed of only a bunk bed, a chair, and two small chests of drawers.

Hyde ushers me through one of the doors. I sit on the bottom bunk. A short head peers over the edge of the top bunk.

"Hey stranger."

By some miraculous oversight or by some devious attempt at proving Sarah unwell, they've assigned us to be roommates.

After Hyde leaves, she climbs down the creaking ladder that leads to the top bunk and rests her head on my shoulder.

"Sarah? What happened?"

She lets out a quivering sigh. "After you left that morning, Aristo and my brother showed up. I don't know what they told them, but my parents disappeared for hours. Then Aristo made me shave my head just because he could. I guess I always wanted short hair, only kept it long because of them, and when my parents got back, he told them I did it myself. Proof of my perversion. Then they put me in the car with a suitcase. I tried to slip away and call you but they followed me, wouldn't even let me go to the bathroom without them waiting outside the door because they thought I'd run away."

I open my mouth, but I can't speak.

I brought this on her. If she hadn't kissed me, if I hadn't kissed her back, if she hadn't somehow fallen in love with me despite everything, then she'd still be safe. But I know that regardless of what either of us could have done, one day, eventually, they would have found us both. So instead of speaking, I just kiss her. She tastes like salt and oranges, as always. She pulls me closer, slips the Christian T-shirt over my head, and straddles me. Then we seriously lapse in our progress toward discovering our inner heterosexual selves.

Afterward I pull my clothes on loosely. I decide to find Leon down the hall. He's clean-shaven, so I think he must have a razor. He's probably the only one here who would enjoy that small act of rebellion. Everyone else seems too scared, too shattered.

Leon answers his door wearing only a pair of hot pink Speedos. "Ahh, friend. I thought you would come see me." He grins toothily. Later he tells me that he refused to let Char and Hyde take them from him. "I said if you do, I won't wear anything at all, will be naked like bear in the winter. Then I danced like this."

He gyrates his hips around, wildly throwing his body out, hands flailing in the air. Apparently they conceded and allowed him to keep his more feminine undergarments.

"I was wondering: Could I borrow something?"

"Hush. Anything for friend." He sweeps his arm out, gestures into the room. I notice the empty top bunk.

"You don't have a roommate?"

He chuckles. "Ha. They didn't trust me with the other boys." He swings his hips around a little. "How does that song go? Too sexy for my vest, too sexy for shoes. Too too sexy." He does jazz hands and chuckles. "I always loved that song. They'd play it in the clubs in Moscow. You know how to dance?"

I nod, unable to keep from smiling.

He grins wider. "Wonderful. I will make you my dance partner."

Leon starts bopping around the room, bringing one hand over his face and making scissor motions. He almost trips a couple of times. I watch him for a few minutes, then, when it becomes clear that if I don't do anything he's not going to stop dancing for me anytime soon, I clear my throat.

"Do you have a razor I could borrow? I want to shave my head so they can't make me wear bows in my hair like they did to the other girls."

"Genius! I never thought of that." He rummages through his chest of drawers and hands me a plastic disposable. "Good luck."

When I turn to leave, he's still dancing, swaying his arms and whisper-singing some garbled version of that song, though instead of getting the lyrics right, he keeps muttering, "Too too sexy, too too. Sexy. For my sexy. Vest. For my sexy sexy. On cat's walk."

I shake my head and wave goodbye.

☒ ☒ ☒

THERE ARE two bathrooms: one at the end of the hall with GIRLS scrawled on the door in pink chalk, one adjacent to the girls' bathroom with BOYS written neatly in blue chalk. I go into the boys' room, start rummaging through the plastic bins with each boy's name on it.

Eventually I find what I'm looking for in Jason's basket: a pair of clippers. I think I hear a door open downstairs, so I run into the girls' room and lock the door. Inside there are two sinks and a window that looks out onto the forest, but other than that, it's exactly the same as the boys' room.

I let my hair down. It nearly reaches my collarbone, the curls messy and my makeup streaked so badly that my features are almost indistinguishable, my face blurred with fear and running concealer. In the cracked mirror, my face is

small and sad-looking, like I'm disappearing into myself. I
look older, wilder. Like someone I'd veer away from if I saw
her on the street.

I plug the clippers in and take a deep breath, bite my lip so
I don't cry. I bite down hard, too hard, and my lip splits a little
bit. I can feel the blood in my mouth and it tastes metallic.
First I buzz the top of my head, push the clippers down firmly
enough that the hair falls away from my scalp cleanly. I buzz
the sides next. Leon's razor is cold in my hands, heavier than
I expected. I lather soap over my head before I start shaving,
sliding the blades along the stubble, and what's left of my
hair disappears. My head is burning, and when I tentatively
put a hand to it, it feels raw. I can feel a few nicks from the
blade, and my scalp stings.

I don't look in the mirror. I don't want to know what I
look like because I know I'll be ugly, and I don't want to add
that to my list of problems. But there was no alternative. If I
hadn't gotten rid of my hair, they would have forced me to
wear their trappings. To put on costumes that I might start
to believe were real.

I run my hand over my scalp.

Finally I can't help myself. When I see myself in the mirror,
I start crying. I don't look like the girl I once was anymore. I
look broken. Still, for the first time in my life, I look like the
girl I really am, not like a girl whose entire life has consisted
of passing unsuccessfully as someone she can never truly
become.

It's almost dark now, and there's a full yellow moon hanging
low in the sky. The bathroom window is too small to climb
out of and the drop from the second story is too far, but there
are windows in the front room downstairs.

I know what I'm going to do.

But first I gather up what was once my hair and throw it out the window. I watch it scatter in the air. I feel lighter. Run a hand over my head again and marvel at the smoothness, at how easily I changed from hiding to, for the first time in my life, being purposefully visible.

I knock on Leon's door, ajar the way I left it, and when there's no answer I push it open. He's asleep on the floor, cradling his pillow, tears still stuck to his eyelashes. He whispers a woman's name, a name I think I heard him say when he talked about his mother. I leave the razor on his desk. Then I bend over, pull his blanket off his bed, and drape it over him. He stirs in his sleep a little. I slip out before he wakes up, closing the door behind me.

Sarah's half-asleep when I get back. She starts when I turn on the light. "Where did you go?" Her mouth falls open when she sees my head. "Oh, Raya."

She sounds like she's going to cry, so I climb up and sit next to her.

"I didn't want them to try to change me."

She nods, and a single tear falls down her cheek.

I take her hands in mine. "Look, I think I figured out how to get out of here, but we've got to do it tonight when there's a full moon. There's a forest outside of the house, and I think if we run through it, we'll eventually get to a highway and then I'll figure out what to do from there."

Sarah doesn't say anything. But she nods again, wiping her eyes.

I jump down and get my backpack, stuff in the clothes I'd unpacked only hours before, pausing only to check that the picture of me and Mom is still there. I touch it, rub the corners of the photo between two fingers for good luck. There are some bottles of water on the chest of drawers, and I add those as well. Sarah packs what little she was able to bring in her suitcase, and I put her stuff in my bag too.

Though everyone's asleep, I tell her to take off her shoes so they don't hear us.

We walk barefoot down the hall. It's dark in the house, but the moon sheds enough light through the windows that we can just make out the shapes of furniture. When we get to the front door, it's locked. There's a padlock above the door handle. I find a window, manage to jam it open, and think that soon we'll be free. But I don't know what we'll do once we are.

It's a short fall to the ground, and we both land on our hands and knees. I can feel rocks scraping my palms but don't let myself worry about it. Then we're running. My heart's beating so hard I can't breathe, but the forest is right there, the trees looming ominously in the moonlight.

We're so close and I'm thinking that I'm saving her, that like Orpheus I found her in hell and now we're leaving for good. We just need to get into the dark of the forest and then we'll be safe. They won't be able to find us in there. By the time it's light, we'll be gone. On our way to somewhere else.

The woods are opening up before us.

We're close and I half whisper, "I love you."

She doesn't reply, just grips my hand tighter and keeps pulling me in the direction of the forest. Suddenly she lets go.

"Raya?" Her voice is panicked. "We need to go back inside now."

I turn and see Char about thirty feet away on the porch, a cigarette in hand, watching us.

My breath catches in my throat. I walk up to her. "Sorry, we just wanted some air." It's obvious that I'm lying, but I don't care.

She just nods.

Suddenly I realize that she's still wearing her riding pants and doctor's coat. Her eyes are stained with half circles of exhaustion, the same color as the cigarette smoke. I exhale shakily. If she's an insomniac, then there's no way we will be able to escape at night. During the day we can't possibly get out without someone seeing where we're going. For the first time since I got here, I know that I'm actually going to have to go through this, that I'm not leaving, that I'm trapped here in hell. Embarrasingly, I start to cry.

It's getting light now, dawn seeping through the corners of the sky like a photograph left in the developer for too long, trapped in the moment before the image disappears. Sarah and I walk back to the house.

Char follows us. She's silent until we reach our room. Before we close the door, she says, "I'm sorry, you know. I didn't want this either."

I don't understand what she's saying, but I think about what she might have meant long into the next day.

Part Four:
The Depths of the
Underworld

I failed to escape. Failed to save Sarah.

That's the first thing I can think when I wake up. I must have slept for only a few minutes. I go outside, my bald head like a giant *fuck you* to everyone, to Grammy for sending me here and to the counselors for thinking that they can break me. Sarah is still asleep. I walk my proudest, gayest strut into the dining room, where everyone is eating Froot Loops and whispering among themselves.

There are supposedly more than seven people here, but I'm starting to get the idea that only Leon, Sarah, Clio, Jason, Michael, Diane, and Karma regularly participate in the activities. And Karma looks like she's about to leave; I can see her standing next to some packed bags by the front door.

Hyde sees me looking around. "Patients who have accepted

Jesus can return to their families," he says. "Patients who have progressed further in their therapies rest during the day."

I decide that I don't want to know what that means or why they need to rest.

Clio is pouring herself a bowl of cereal. She glances up, winks at me, mouths "nice hair."

Leon whoops, "This one, she's a cracker-fire!"

After breakfast Leon joins me on the porch swing. He looks at me sideways.

"You know here, they try to break you, but if you just pretend it's a dream, it'll be okay. I like to think of it as big gay party. Or summer camp. When I get out of here, I'm going to start a club." His eyes sparkle. "For people like us. And I'll play the 'too sexy' song every night, like they did at that place in Moscow. It was called Scissors and I think it was for the muffin eaters, but I went anyway."

I wonder if Leon knows he's getting American slang wrong, but I don't correct him, just let him dream about his club.

When Leon and I go back inside, I see her. I watch her drinking the coffee that she talked Hyde into giving her. She told him she gets migraines and it's the only thing that helps, though really she just likes how bitter it is, how it makes her teeth ache. She likes it better when coffee grinds fall into her mug and she can feel their grit on her tongue with each sip.

In the morning light her eyes always look gray. Today her short hair is fuzzy and so scruffy and sad-looking that it gives her the air of a sick baby bird.

Outside she rips off the pink clip and gives Char a look, like she's daring her to say anything. Char just looks down at her cigarette; she's let it burn down so far that it's singeing her fingers.

I wince, holding my breath.

When Char notices me noticing the burns, she only brushes the ash off, ignoring the raw welts already rising up on her hand.

Leon says that Char uses experimental injections and pills that are designed to drug us into heterosexuality. Says she can't sleep because of her own experience with the therapy, which is why she smokes and drinks so much coffee, like she's trying to chemically compensate for however her body doesn't function right. Says that she works here because she herself had been converted by this camp and apparently was converted to the point that she decided to devote her life to saving the young homosexuals and transsexuals of America. He whispers in my ear, "My father told me that Hyde's father put him and Char in charge because he didn't think they could make it in the outside world. That he had the church buy this place years ago, but he signed it over to Hyde. The checks go to Hyde's father, I saw the one mine sent. This whole thing, like smoke screen. Stacked against us."

Friendly Saviors saves the kids in it by enforcing two activities. The first is making them perform pointless acts of menial labor every day. I learn this from Clio, who doesn't specify the labor. I assume she means we have to play sports.

She leans in so that her mouth is next to my ear and says, so quietly that I almost don't hear her, "I saw you two leaving last night. Don't ever try to get out by yourself again. There isn't really a way, unless there are more than a couple kids. Getting caught will only make it worse for you. If you need to, just pretend it's working. I pretend to date Jason, though he doesn't know I'm pretending. It works because I only have to talk to him when they're around, and they give me more privileges and stopped reading my mail."

Clio smiles. "I've got a girl back at college. Her name's Iris. She's a painter. We met in school, before my parents found out. As soon as I can find a way out of here, I'm gone."

I consider telling her about Sarah and me, but decide it's too dangerous and just nod and say nothing. Instead I study the schedule written on a whiteboard hanging over the table. After breakfast we have exercise, which lasts for four hours, and then lunch, a prayer/confession circle, individual meetings with counselors, free time, and then more exercise. Dinner, another prayer circle, and then we have what is left of the evening to ourselves. The board is divided by names. Sarah, Leon, Clio, Maia (Michael), Jason, and I all got the top.

At the bottom, though, there's a list of names of people who, except for Diane, I haven't met. All they have are three treatments per day, "recovery," and an individual meeting with Hyde. I swallow the lump in my throat that tells me their treatments aren't going to be something you can recover from.

Hyde stands up. "It's time, everyone."

  🀆 🀆 🀆

I WALK outside, thinking we're going to go running or play ball, only to find thirteen wheelbarrows—each filled with small boulders. The rocks are about the size of basketballs, the kind of rocks that the wealthier people in Pieria use to line their driveways and gardens. It turns out that "exercise" is lifting each boulder, carrying it across an empty football field, then going back to pick up another boulder—again and again until the wheelbarrow is empty. It's as if they want to exhaust the gay out of our bodies, as if it were something that can be beaten into submission.

I pick up the first boulder, trying not to outwardly show the pain of its weight in my arms, and walk as proudly as I can to try to prove something to Grammy, to Hyde. I speed up until I'm half running, and I finish the boulder moving before everyone else. I think that now I'll get to go inside and lie down. Instead Hyde wheels the empty wheelbarrow back to me.

"Now put them all back in and do it again."

The Texas sun is beating down on me like a bruise and I can feel the skin on my face and scalp burning. My arms ache so badly I think they might be splitting open. But I won't let myself grimace, scared that Hyde—or worse, Char, who's perched at the edge of the field on a lawn chair, still smoking one of her ever-present cigarettes—will sense my pain and my weakness and exploit it.

I start the long and terrible task of carrying the boulders back. Like Sisyphus, I think my rock moving will never end, that I'll die with my arms broken, that even in my death I'll be carrying the boulders' weight. But finally I reach the last rock. I can't look at Sarah, don't want her to see the exhaustion breaking across my face like hives.

I walk inside with sore arms that feel they've been turned to nothing.

We all file into the kitchen. There, we're given dry peanut

butter sandwiches with moldy-tasting bread. Then we're led back to our prayer circle. As we take our places, I try to watch Sarah for any signs that all of this is working. What the signs would be, I don't know. I only see the sunburn spreading out across her shoulders in red patches.

When it's my turn to go, I talk about all the years I spent in hiding, trying to be straight. In my new version of events, I had a fake boyfriend who was also gay, and a girlfriend named Mariana who wanted to be a dancer and had eyes so green they looked blue. I tell the group that it never went further than us holding hands because she moved to New York City to chase her dream of being a prima ballerina.

When I'm done, Char says I'm possessed with something unholy, that I am dirty, infected with the filth of hell. She says it was because I had no mom that I turned out this way.

Then Hyde sets in, though his tone is gentler than Char's, Grammy must have told them about the wings, because he says that my wings are devil-spawned, proof that I'm twisted, that something was wrong with me from the day I entered this world. He tells me that whenever I feel my old ways coming back, I should visualize what will happen to me if I can't allow myself to be saved—how hell will claim me like it claimed so many other queers.

As they're saying these things, I have to remind myself that I'm not disgusting like they say, that there's nothing really wrong with me.

While it's happening, I avoid looking at Sarah and meet her gaze only when they've moved on to Jason—who confesses that sometimes he wishes he'd never been born at all. They tell him that if he's going to live in sin, maybe he shouldn't have. Jason covers his mouth with a shaking hand, and in the light his skin is so sallow that it's as translucent as paper.

When they get to Clio, she rolls her eyes.

"I got here because I met this girl, Iris, and we got together. You know, anywhere but Texas, two girls together is basically a normal thing. My parents opened a letter she sent me when I was home from college for the summer, and that's how they found out and sent me here. It's wrong, I know now that I'm ready to rejoin the outside world, but I love her"—she glances at Jason and quickly corrects herself—"*loved* her, that is. I love Jason now that we've both made such progress together."

Hyde nods. "Very good, Clio. But remember, it's not normal."

Sarah's staring at me, her eyes wild, and it takes me a minute to realize that she's afraid.

I can't go to her, so I stare back until they've finished the circle, until everyone has stood up, and we're the only ones still seated, holding the pocket Bibles they make us open at the beginning and end of every session.

⊞　⊞　⊞

AFTER THAT, I have my first private meeting with Char. We walk to her office in an uncomfortable silence. The room is covered in books with titles like *Homosexuality: The Truth Behind the Mental Illness*, and although she's still wearing the same pair of tan riding pants and her coat is stained at the sleeves with flakes of tobacco, she has showered. A pencil holds her silver-white hair in a twisted bun. It's still wet, leaving little droplets on her jacket.

I sit down at the mahogany desk, which looks older than

the both of us. The top has long, catlike scratches on the surface. I notice framed pictures at the edge: one is of a young Char posing with a horse.

The room is dusty, books strewn over the floor. I feel the pit drop out of my stomach when I see a bowl full of ice, a bowl of steaming water, and a small silver device with clips that look like they attach to your fingers. Briefly and irrationally I think that she's going to kill me, that I'll be murdered and nobody will ever know, that my body will never leave this place. She won't tell anyone, and Sarah will think that I ran away and left her here alone. Grammy will think that I just ran away, that I left everyone and my one shot at a normal life behind.

Char begins by showing me pictures of two girls holding hands. One of the girls has cropped hair and is wearing a man's button-down. The other has long brown hair and a pink silk blouse. The girl with the cropped hair reminds me of Sarah, and when I see them I can't help smiling a little bit, and that's when she dips my fingers into the freezing water. The cold's a shocking burn, and instead of looking away I smile wider in the direction of the pictures. I smile so wide that my mouth hurts and I know that I look crazy. She pushes my hands deeper into the freezing water and it makes my eyes well, but I blink back the tears and make myself start laughing.

In a movement so fast I don't register it until it's happened, Char pulls my hands out—upending the bowl and spilling ice and water everywhere, smearing her papers and notes with water stains—and twists my arm behind my back.

After that, Char marches me outside. She takes me to the football field and lets me go so suddenly that I fall. Then she sits down in the lawn chair and orders me to carry three wheelbarrows' worth of rocks back and forth.

I think about saying no.

But I remember the list of names at the bottom of the whiteboard and the small electric machine on her desk. So I decide that my name won't be at the bottom of the list in the kitchen today, and I pick up the first boulder.

Soon my vision is blurring and my arms burn. I see Sarah watching me from the window until it looks like someone pulls her away to her own therapy session. If it's with Hyde she's probably better off, or at least that's what I tell myself. I pick up another boulder and then another, and I keep going until eventually my vision begins to turn black and then dissolves into nothing.

The thing about nice homophobes is that they're the worst kind of homophobe. They'll smile at you on the street, maybe say that it would be okay if everyone could get married, but wouldn't it undermine the sanctity of marriage if the gays could too? They lull you into a false sense of security and make you feel safe enough that you'll let your guard down, and for a moment maybe entertain the idea of dropping your disguise. And then they metaphorically cut your throat.

I learned the type when I was in middle school: the girls who invite you over to dinner, girls whose parents will talk politics at the dinner table and say things about how they don't mind gay people as long as they don't have to see them or interact with them. They applaud themselves for their tolerance but vote for politicians who want to make gayness a mental illness again, then smile at you at church the next day. With every action they make to take away your rights, they adopt an air of phony shame, as if they actually cared about the consequences of their beliefs.

So when I wake up to Hyde wrapping a blanket around me, gently putting a thermometer under my tongue, asking how I'm feeling, I'm suspicious.

Sometimes I think it's almost better when they outright tell you they hate you, when you know what to expect from the beginning. With men like Hyde, men who smile too kindly and act all fatherly while trying to erase your identity, the line between safe and not safe blurs in a way that scares me.

Rosie from school was like that. When she saw me with Sarah, she became afraid of me in a way that I didn't know was possible coming from her, but that I had always been scared would happen. I was always just so afraid. Afraid that someone would look at me with the kind of fear and recognition that turns into gay teens disappearing to places like this and ends with them never leaving, never becoming anything other than trapped inside their own gay bodies.

My vision is still blurry. Other than the strange anxiety buzzing in my chest, I'm not sure what happened. I remember falling. I think I hit my head. The images come back disjointed: the heels of Char's tan leather boots digging into the grass. Hands around my shoulders, pulling me up. The rock falling out of my arms and landing on the ground. A sharp pain in the back of my skull. Then nothing.

I lean back on the couch in the nurse's quarters, an area now run by Char—after the nurse apparently had a midlife crisis and quit last year, leaving behind everything but the empty planters in the windowsills. Weirdly, the nurse didn't bother to bring the pots with her, and from my position on the couch, I can see the cracked terra-cotta forms that cast long and ominous shadows on the floor. I close my eyes, let the shadows melt back into nothingness.

Before I wake up, I hear Sarah's voice and forget where I am. I think it's another morning when the night before was still a half-answered question and Sarah was waiting for me to wake up, sitting at the edge of her big metal bed with two mugs of black coffee (both hers) and watching me. Those mornings, she'd never do anything to wake me up even though she got up hours before I did. She would just sit and drink her coffee and wait for me before doing anything to start her day.

Still, in the space between consciousness and not, I remember the dream I had: she and I were in an ocean and the tide kept pulling me under. She was wearing a white hospital gown, and my wings had returned. She called out, "Stop struggling; you'll sink faster." But I couldn't stop, and soon the salty water was filling my throat and seeping into my lungs. I clawed at my mouth but I couldn't breathe. My wings were too water-logged to fly and hung limp and heavy from my back. Sarah was gone. And then I started to sink. Suddenly I felt her arms around me, pulling me out. But when we beached on the sand, I couldn't feel my wings. When I put a hand to my back, there was only wet, empty skin.

She whispered, "I had to cut them off; they weighed you down too much."

I wake up gasping, like I always do when I have dreams about my wings returning.

Then Sarah is there, sitting next to me, and I remember everything.

Hyde and Char are gone and we are alone. She puts her hands on my shoulders. "You scared me. Don't do that again."

I kiss her, feel the tears drying on her cheeks. "Don't cry."

She doesn't say anything, just kisses me harder until we hear footsteps coming down the hall and pull away from each other. She hurls herself into the chair on the other side of the room and manages to slump down in it in a way that looks almost natural before the door opens.

Hyde walks in. "Raya? You can leave now. You fainted, but Char checked you out and gave you a clean bill." He grins, and it's almost goofy in a way that makes me hate him even more. "Be careful about carrying those rocks from now on. We can't have any more accidents. I had to go to town to pick up these electrolyte waters, and Char says that if you drink a couple bottles every few hours, you'll be good. Mainly you're just dehydrated . . ."

He keeps droning on, but I'm not listening because I have realized something: the truck in the driveway. He must take it out on supply runs fairly regularly, and if he does, that means he keeps the keys somewhere close by—or better yet, they're in his pocket.

I glance at Sarah, but she doesn't seem to understand.

Eventually I start to nod and ask if I could have one of the waters, just to get him to stop talking. When he walks over to hand me the bottle, his left pocket jingles. He's wearing those old, baggy jeans—made for a much bigger man, but that men like him wear and they think they're cool even though their jeans look like the pants the bingo-playing grandmas wear. He constantly hitches them up, so the pockets gape open like an apron: easy to steal from without the wearer noticing.

I smile too brightly and give him back the bottle with the fluorescent blue liquid in it.

"Hyde? Sorry, could you open this for me? I can't get it."

While he's struggling to get the cap off, I slip a hand in his pants pocket and grab the keys.

Sarah's watching. Her eyes widen when she sees the flash of metal disappearing into my skirt's compartment-pocket thing.

The skirts here are true atrocities with kangaroo-like pouches built into them. I think the pouches are meant to carry pocket Bibles. Mine carry sugar packets to eat in the privacy of our room later. Clio saw me taking the packets from the kitchen, and for a second I worried she'd tell someone, but she just laughed.

"That's a good idea; sometimes you need a little sweetness."

At lunch when nobody was looking, she slipped an open packet into my hand, winking at me. I turned and let the granules dissolve into a gritty sweetness on my tongue, and just for a second, I felt better.

🔲 🔲 🔲

I'VE STOLEN only once before, when I was twelve.

I'd gotten my period for the first time, and although I didn't really understand what the dark mass of blood staining my pants meant, I knew that I was supposed to buy a box of sanitary pads. But I didn't have any money on me and I didn't want to tell Grammy. I didn't want to hear her sigh and watch her get misty-eyed while she took care of me but thought about my mother and her girlhood, a girlhood that had disappeared, like mine disappeared—though mine was spent in hiding and Mom's was spent being too visible.

All I ever was to Grammy was a girl raised in the place of my mother's shadow. A consolation prize. Whenever I hit any kind of milestone on my way to womanhood (getting breasts and buying my first bra, getting hips, getting a note in the mailbox from some boy, something that clearly thrilled Grammy and irritated me), she treated them as stepping-stones on the way to prevent me from becoming my mother—as ways to tamp down the girl inside me, to kill every part that reminds her in a bad way of my mom. To create instead the perfect substitute: a girl who resembles her in every way except the undesirable, wilder ones. And we both knew it, though neither of us ever said anything, except once when I was half-asleep on the couch. She shook me awake, and said, "We have to go to church."

But she called me Calli.

I said, "I'm not her, you know."

Grammy bit her lip and said, "I know," but the way she said it, we both knew that she didn't.

I never tried to address it, always just thought that one day maybe Mom would come back and I'd stop having to be her replacement, a knockoff version of her.

The day I got my period, I rode my bike out to the convenience store. Sarah met me there to distract Jonathan, the man who worked at the register on Sunday afternoons, while I slipped the box into my backpack—almost knocking over a Twinkies display in the process. Back at Sarah's house,

I tried to wash the blood out of my pants but couldn't. I got in the shower with my clothes on and turned the water on high so Sarah wouldn't hear me crying. It was moments like that when my mother's absence hurt more than I could stand, when a deep longing for all the things I'd never known took root in my belly and stayed there.

Sarah must have been listening outside the door because she came in and got in the shower with me and held me until I stopped sobbing. She dried me off, taught me how to put on the wings of the pads so they wouldn't bunch up.

Then she slapped my face.

I thought it was because she knew that the week before, I'd learned that I was truly gay, though I'd known, deep down, for a long time. I'd told no one and changed nothing about my appearance or demeanor, but I was paranoid that everyone could sense it. I turned away from Sarah, the realization that I'd been found out slowly sinking into me. But then she laughed.

"Sorry. My mom said that my grandma slapped her after she got her period, and that my great-grandma did too, and so on. It's some kind of family tradition. She slapped me when I got mine. I think it's supposed to be good luck."

I was so relieved that I muttered, "Thank you."

Then I put on some of Sarah's clothes, and we walked loops around her block until night fell and her parents were calling for us to return.

☷ ☷ ☷

NOW WE'RE walking down the corridor to our second group prayer circle of the day. I think of how Hyde explained to Grammy that one of their techniques is having a twice-daily prayer circle where the patients confess some kind of sin to the rest of the campers. (It feels like it's been weeks since she left me on the porch and I watched the green Volvo speed away, driving so fast she almost ran over the welcome sign.) What he didn't tell her is that if one of the patients doesn't have a sin to confess, the staff refuses to feed them or doubles their physical labor for the day.

I tell myself that I won't confess to anything, that I won't let them make me pretend to become someone else, but I know it's only a matter of time before they break me down. I know I'll have to pretend to have become another person, a straight girl—and while I know they can't make me straight, I'm afraid I'll begin to believe them when they tell me I'm wrong, doomed.

I have the keys to get away, and as long as Hyde doesn't look for them or put his hand in his pocket and notice that they're gone, I'm safe. As Sarah and I enter the room, I decide to say that the month before I got found out, I kissed a girl in the darkness of the school's photography room while we waited for the pictures we'd taken for an art assignment to develop. My real school doesn't have an art room, but Hyde and Char don't know that. In the fake life of the fake girl I've decided to pretend to be, it's true.

In reality, my first kiss was in the bathroom after my seventh-grade dance with a girl named Dani. She just grabbed me, knocking her teeth against mine in the process. Then she let me go and walked out, slamming the bathroom door. I just stood there gasping.

I ran after her, wanted to ask her not to tell anyone, thinking it was some kind of test the other girls had put her up to, to prove my dykehood, but she just flashed me a peace sign and walked off. She never spoke to me again. The next summer she was found kissing the other girl who got outed at prom. That night in the bathroom was the last time I saw her.

⊞ ⊞ ⊞

THE GROUP starts. The kids who are "resting" are still gone, secluded somewhere. As we all get settled, I notice that Jason and Michael both look legitimately terrified. Jason's voice shakes as he says—in the same tone you would use to admit to committing murder—that he thought about holding hands with a man today, though only for a couple of seconds, and that afterward he went into the bathroom and ran cold water and dipped his hands into it in an attempt to mimic Char's treatments.

The two saddest things about this place are seeing campers confess the most mundane parts of their queerness as if they were speaking to God himself, and seeing the "cured" patients come up with false sins.

Michael says that today he tried to pull his bra around his body but pulled it so tight he couldn't breathe, so for a few minutes he had a makeshift binder. And briefly, what he saw reflected back in the bathroom mirror was who he actually is, or at least as close to being himself as he can get in a place like this.

Hyde puts a hand on Michael's shoulder. "Maia, you need to accept your body and its purpose, to be a wife, a mother, a servant of the Lord, and only when you do will you find peace. But accepting yourself, your purpose, is the only way to salvation."

Tears are welling in Michael's eyes, and Hyde kneels down so they're at eye level. "You'll return to the path that you strayed from. God will find you, Maia."

Michael won't meet his eyes, just stares fixedly at the floor.

Clio says that she thought of a girl she slept with the summer before her senior year of high school. The girl got married to her high school sweetheart shortly after, had a new baby before graduation, turned bright red and started stammering whenever she saw Clio in the halls, a protective hand held tight over her rounding belly. Hyde says that Clio needs to save herself like the girl did. "That girl, she recognized something sour in her, lurking beneath the surface, and she fixed it with something sweet. She fulfilled what she was always meant to be. And now you're working to do the same."

Leon says he misses "beautiful blond-haired boys."

Char snaps at him, "That isn't a confession."

Leon thinks for a minute. "Boys who I want to make naked?" he adds, and Char nods.

Hyde then starts in on how Leon was too close to his mother growing up, and because she raised him when his father was away, Leon grew inward—became womanly, got confused, tempted by the wrong forces. Leon smirks while Hyde says this, but I notice that his hands are shaking.

Then it's my turn.

When I speak, my voice shakes too, for reasons I don't entirely understand. "Um, well, last year I was in the darkroom at school, developing pictures for my art assignment, and the girl I had the assignment with, Lana, kissed me." I trail off, blushing. Admitting my gayness out loud—even when I'm lying—is still strange. Even though I've been found, I'm not used to being seen. My heart starts beating too fast and I can feel my cheeks flushing hotter as everyone continues to look at me. Sarah raises an eyebrow at me. I shrug back at her.

Char turns to me, and her eyes are icy, sphinxlike. In this light she's so cold and pale it looks like she could be made out of marble. Her face has the same delicate fleshy quality as all those Greek sculptures I've seen pictures of—as if she's flickering between being dead and not.

"And what did you do?"

"I kissed her back."

She smiles almost imperceptibly and turns away.

Hyde says, "Admitting sin is the first step toward healing. Eventually, Raya, the life you led will seem like nothing more than a nightmare, a bad dream meant to test you. But you can wake up from this."

I nod, swallow hard.

Sarah's next.

Looking at her, I think about that night she kissed me, about how she started to cry again after I kissed her back. "Raya? I'm scared." How I held her against me and said that nothing would happen to either of us, even though we both knew it would. How I promised her that we'd both be safe. But that promise was broken. All I can do now is try to get her out of here.

She sighs. "Earlier, I guess I thought about women."

Char starts to open her mouth, but Hyde puts a hand over hers, turns to Sarah. "What did you think about that was sinful?"

Sarah's got a sort of glimmer in her eyes that I've never seen before, something between terror and rebellion.

"I thought about fucking them. I don't know about you, Hyde, but I just love when you're going down on a girl and her thighs start to shake. Though you probably wouldn't know about it from firsthand experience."

Hyde is clenching and unclenching his hands into fists. "Those are sinful things, Sarah. It's not the Lord that's causing you to behave in this way."

I make frantic knife motions under my throat, hoping that she'll stop, that she'll save herself, but she ignores me and forges on.

"The last girl called for the Lord when I was done with her. Did that ever happen to you, Char?"

Char's face has morphed into a strange mask, her eyes eerily still, and she grabs Sarah's arm, yanks her up, and half drags her outside. Hyde starts, like he's going to stop Char, then changes his mind, hangs back and watches. The only person who took the punishment silently when they said that though he'd told them his thoughts he still wouldn't get dinner was Jason, but I think he's been starved for so long that he has forgotten how to be hungry. He's forgotten all about the outside world away from Friendly Saviors. All he has is shame and fear.

I abandon all attempts at hiding what Sarah means to me and run after her and Char—not caring, in that moment, that they'll realize we know each other and that since neither of us lived anywhere other than Pieria and both of us arrived at the same time, we're together and had something to do with each other's disappearances.

☷　☷　☷

WHAT DO they see when they look at us?

Sarah's hair is still ragged, but she carries herself with a strange regality, like she's locked her body inside itself. She wears the long denim peasant skirts that make us look like Mormon fortune-tellers and the tucked-in shirts that have off-brand Christian slogans on them with the same butch bravado as she once wore her baggy men's pants and frayed white tank tops.

My head's shaved, and I've been trying my best not to look in mirrors, but I know that without the wildly tangled curls hiding my face, I look just like my mother. I have her small features and high bone structure, only I'm younger and darker-haired and sadder-looking in some intangible way. I wear the uniform slightly less gracefully than Sarah does, with the ends of my long shirt tied behind my back and the skirt dragging at my ankles.

I've spent so much time trying to hide my body because of its desires that I've never thought about whether I'm attractive. When I was younger, I would wear the loosest shirts I could find to hide my breasts, and pants three sizes too big that I'd hold up by cinching the belt loops around my waist with scarves. Though Grammy started buying me tight sundresses, I still tried to hide my body under oversized jackets, long scarves, and unpadded bras several sizes too small that left red half-moon marks under my ribs when I took them off.

The only time I thought my body could be beautiful to someone else was the first time I slept with Sarah. As she unzipped my dress, she kissed the scars where the vertebrae had broken through my skin, and I knew from what I saw in her eyes that when she looked at the scars, when she looked at my body, she saw something I had never been able to see when I stood in front of the mirror: she saw something desirable.

If they look closely enough, maybe they can see the slight bumps that are different from the natural curvature of a spine under my shirt. The possibility of flight that was ripped out of me, the silvery marks that are all that's left of that hollow promise now. And if they look even closer, they can see that I try not to look at Sarah directly. If they keep looking, they will see the motherless sadness that I keep mostly hidden.

⊞   ⊞   ⊞

THE OTHERS follow me. Char's leading Sarah to the edge of the football field. She looks at Sarah with her mouth set into a thin line, a look that I know from my time with Grammy means trouble.

"Run," Char tells her. "Don't stop until I tell you to."

And so Sarah, resigned to whatever happens to her, runs. Char makes her run for two hours, until the sun is low in the sky and the crickets have started to sound. Eventually she keeps falling down and taking so long to get back up that my heart thuds in my throat. Her skin is flushed, wet with sweat, and in the rippling light her sunburn looks like it's catching fire, like she's being set aflame. When she falls, Char just calls out "faster," and then she's a blur of a girl in motion again.

While she runs, I hold the keys in my hand so tightly that I can feel them cutting into my skin. Our freedom. Char won't be sleeping, will still be on the porch, but with a car it won't matter. There's only one vehicle here, and she couldn't follow us very far on foot. As long as we can get in the car and lock the doors before she reaches us, we'll be safe. I'll ask Leon to come with us and tell him to bring Clio, too. I don't know if I can completely trust them, but I know it would be better to have more than two escapees. Harder to catch all of us. Besides, Clio stole the sugar for me, risked the wrath of Char, who presides over the kitchen supplies, so she seems trustworthy.

Sarah's slowing down now and I can see her chest heaving. Her legs are shaking. Her shirt is covered with a deep V of sweat, and I can tell she's starting to give up and my stomach hurts, but I can't do anything now without making it worse for her.

At the end of the two hours, Char turns to go inside, to start dinner and preside over the quiet table, and everyone leaves with her, with slightly guilty but too-scared-to-do-anything expressions on their faces.

I go to Sarah. She's gasping, doubled over. I sit down next to her in the grass and hold her head in my lap as she cries. Then she sits up. She has a strange look on her face, and at first I think she's going to say something to me, but then she throws up. I pull my sleeve down over my arm and wipe her mouth, hold her tighter because it's all that I can really do.

We stay like this until the moon is out.

She looks at me, finally. "We need to leave. Tonight."

I nod, slip the keys out of my pocket, and hand them to her. She manages to stand up, though she's limping, and I bring her around to the back of the house where no one will see us and then up to our room, where I make her lie down.

🚪 🚪 🚪

WHEN I go into the kitchen, everyone's quiet. Watching me. I know bringing two plates would look suspicious, so I heap one plate with too much food.

Hyde decided to let Jason and Michael eat after all. Tonight dinner is canned vegetables that long ago lost their vegetable-ness and are now just indistinguishable brown pieces of something spongy-looking. There's corn bread, chicken (slightly raw on the inside but burnt on the outside), and lukewarm milk. It's clear that Char is the one who cooked it because she watches everyone eat, gets a vaguely violent expression whenever she notices anyone trying not to grimace or spitting food into their napkins.

I whisper that I don't feel well, that my head's still ringing, and surprisingly Char lets me leave. Upstairs I set the food down in front of Sarah. She eats it quickly, keeps offering me some, but I can't eat because my throat feels like it's closed up. She puts the keys on the bed between us. In the dark of the room, the metal of the keys almost glows, and I realize I'm slightly afraid of touching them, like they're some kind of weapon. Then there's a knock on the door, and I put the keys in my skirt's pocket, hope Hyde hasn't figured out they're missing yet.

But it's just Leon. He's leaning in the doorway. "You feeling better?"

Sarah nods.

He smiles at me. "The bald looks good on you."

I've made up my mind. "Here, close the door."

He raises an eyebrow but comes to sit next to us on the bed.

I pull the keys out from under the mattress. "They're to the truck. We're going to get out tonight. Do you want to come?"

Leon sucks his teeth so hard I can hear them crack, shakes his head. At first I worry he's going to tell the others, that I was wrong to tell him and I just ruined our only chance at escape. But then he chuckles. "You're sly, Rainy. I'm going to call you that now"—he traces around my eyes with his index finger—"because your eyes always look like you just cried."

He turns to Sarah. "I'll call you Birdy, because you run like a girl who could fly." She smiles at him but doesn't say anything.

Suddenly he looks serious. "But what will we do when we get out?"

"I don't know yet; I just know we need to leave here. We'll figure it out after." I stare at him. "Leon? Do you trust Clio?"

"Of course."

"Tell her to come too."

He grins again and jumps up, hurrying out. "Wait."

A few minutes later he comes back holding four socks that look like they've been stuffed with something. He tosses them on the floor, and something in the socks clangs. "I put these in the lining of my suitcase. I thought when Papa told me he was taking me here, he meant jail. So I sewed these in."

We pull out rolls of coins. They're all silver dollars. I don't know how he even got them since I thought they stopped making them years ago. I look at the socks. Each one is worth about a hundred bucks.

"Is this enough?" I whisper.

"More than."

He gets up, says he'll meet us downstairs at one in the morning.

As he's leaving, Char knocks on the door.

"Girls?"

I push the socks under the blankets on the top bunk, hoping she didn't notice. "What?"

She sits down on the floor. "Look, I'm sorry about earlier—to both of you. Sometimes I don't know when to stop." She seems legitimately upset. Her pale eyes—eyes that look almost completely white—are watery with tears that could be real or crocodile. "I don't know. My mother always said I needed to be more careful. I just sometimes can't find the line between good or not."

I don't want to say anything, but Sarah looks upset, touches her shoulder.

"Did you go here too?"

Her features sharpen, the sadness gone, replaced with the mask. The shift is startling, like watching an afternoon suddenly shift to the blank darkness of night.

"It doesn't matter. Good night, girls."

She leaves, slamming the door behind her.

When I first got here, I swore to myself that they couldn't break me. But now I sense small fissures in the cracks of my selfhood. It's only been two days—already I feel like I'm losing the memory of the girl I once was. I have no choice. I'm going to either get out or die here.

Sarah and I sit in silence, waiting for the house to go quiet. Eventually, just before one in the morning, everything is silent. We put our pillows under our blankets, drape the sheets around them so that in the dark of the room, they look like they could be our sleeping bodies.

Leon creaks the door open. "Ready? Clio's waiting. Her room's at the end of the hall."

We follow him. He knocks softly and Clio answers. She's wearing what is clearly someone else's shirt. Guessing by the way she carefully pulls the sleeves over her wrists like it's something precious, it probably belongs to the girl she left behind.

He says, "Girl, get your things. We're blowing joint."

"Blowing this joint," I correct Leon, pulling the keys out of my pocket.

Sarah laughs, covers her mouth with her hand.

Clio whispers, "Let me get my things. I had to wait until Diane was asleep."

While she packs, we move her blankets around too. By the time they realize we're not here, that the shapes in our beds are not our sleeping bodies, it will be dawn and we'll be gone, already on our way to freedom.

We walk through the dark house. Everything is silent. Leon opens the door to the kitchen, and we slip out of the house and walk around the yard to the front, where the truck is parked.

Char's smoking on the porch, but she's got a faraway look in her eyes, like she's not in her own body. And we have the keys to the truck, so we have the advantage.

I point to her slumped form.

"We just need to run. The car is at the end of the driveway. Lock the doors once everyone's in, and she won't be able to do anything."

Then we're running, faster than I've ever run before. The mud in the driveway has dried up, and it turns to dust under our feet. We get to the truck. It's unlocked.

Everyone's in and I click the locks. Last year Grammy took me out to a field on the outskirts of Pieria and taught me how to drive the Volvo, and I can't help but remember her lessons now, how her fingers trembled as she handed me the keys.

In the rearview mirror, I see Char walking toward us. I can't get the truck to start because my hands are shaking too much to get the key in the ignition, and panic is rising in my throat. I think for a moment that we're done, it's over. I hold my breath.

But Char raps on the window. She says, "I don't have to tell anyone what I saw for three hours." Then she walks back to the house. In the moonlight, her almost-white skin glows.

I finally get the key in the ignition, start the truck. I floor the gas pedal as hard as I can, and we careen out of the driveway. The forest looms strangely, the moon is high and bright tonight, but the trees block out the light, making it hard to see. I white-knuckle the steering wheel and try not to veer. Something (a deer, I think) runs across the road. I swerve crazily to avoid it and lose control.

I see the crash before I feel our bodies being thrown against the dashboard, the airbag exploding against my chest. I'm outside my body watching the four of us.

There's blood on my face and Sarah's eyes are closed.

Clio and Leon seem fine, but they are upside down. No, the truck is upside down in the road. I don't know how. Someone is saying something, and it takes me a long time to realize it's my name. Then I feel a sharp pain in my back, and in my haze I think that it's my wings, that they have finally returned to me.

Part Five:
A Girl at
the Edge

When I wake up, all I can see is light. It burns my eyes. It takes me a few minutes to realize it's a flashlight, that the car skidded out and flipped over, and everyone at Friendly Saviors heard the crash and came to save us. That I failed again. That we are trapped here with no way of getting out. Sarah's arm is twisted out and her nose is bloody. She's so pale it looks like all the blood was drained from her, and I'm so scared she's dead, that it's my fault. I put my hand over her mouth and feel her breath. She's alive.

I'm still half-upside down, caught from the seat belt.

Then everything goes black again.

I wake up in a cot in a drab room that I've never seen before. There are three cots next to mine. I can see Sarah's ragged head, Clio's twists, and Leon's black hair, blue in the morning light. I sit up fast, thinking at first that we've escaped, that we're free, that I imagined the crash. Then I see Char in the corner of the room.

Char stands up, wipes her palms on her pants, leaving sweat marks. She's nervous, something I didn't think possible since she usually seems more robot than woman.

"Raya?"

"Yes?"

Then it hits me: I know where we are. We're in the second house. The house where they send the kids who spend all their time resting or wandering around vacantly. Kids whose faces always look like drawings before they're erased from the paper completely: only melting shadows in the space of what they once were and what they could have been had they not been disappeared.

"Do you remember what happened?"

I don't know what to say or how to prevent what I know is coming, so I just shake my head.

Char sits down next to me on the cot, which creaks under her weight. She looks down at me and her lips twitch a little bit, as if the shadow of a smile were crossing her face. "I knew a girl like you once."

"What happened to her?"

She sighs. "I don't know. She got out."

"Like I tried to?"

Her face softens. "You know, it's better this way. To be like me. Cured."

"But are you?" My head aches still, and there's a low ringing in my ears.

The softness disappears and she stands up brusquely. "Of course I am. Anyway, given your recent behaviors, we have to treat the four of you accordingly." She pauses, then shakes her head. "After you've eaten, I have to start. Hyde's orders."

I realize we're all going on the list at the bottom of the whiteboard.

■■■   ■■■   ■■■

SARAH IS awake now. She's fine except for a bruised arm. The others, amazingly, are unharmed as well. I decide to wait until later to tell them about whatever is going to happen to us. We walk to the main house. Michael and Diane watch us nervously but say nothing. They give us bowls of instant oatmeal and cups of lukewarm water to drink.

When Jason sees us, his eyes widen. "You're getting the electric shock treatments?"

Sarah turns to me, but I don't have to say anything. She can already see it on my face. Her bottom lip quivers as we sit down. I reach for her hand under the table, and it's shaking. I hold it, run my thumb over the base of the vein at her wrist, feel it pump quickly against my hand. She smiles at me, though her smile is forced.

So far all they've done is make us go to group prayer circles where we have to share our sexual experiences or urges, or if we have nothing to share, to make up some psychosexual bullshit. Then they make us move rocks. Then there was the first therapy session where Char showed me photos of beautiful women together and put my hands in cold water, held them there until I could feel the skin around my fingertips shrivel, go numb with pain.

Apparently the idea is for us to develop a "natural" aversion to our gayness, so we'll only be able to remember our sexuality as pain. But when that doesn't work, there's the next step. I'm afraid. Of what the electroshock therapy will be like. I'm scared they'll fry me so completely that I lose everything: Sarah, my memories, my mind.

Clio told me that when they get really desperate for results, they drug you. Administer meds in illegally high doses for disorders you don't have, until you're nothing, neither gay nor trans nor straight.

Char leads me to a windowless room with three chairs, a cot, and a metal examination table. There's a small chest of drawers and then a machine and a tray next to it with some wires that have little attachments like suction cups on the ends.

The door is open and I could run, but I have nowhere to go, no money, no one to call, the truck's crashed, and I'm too tired to run anymore; I just can't. I know now that it's all over.

Char instructs me to lie down on the table. She wheels the machine over and straps my arms in.

Sarah and Leon and Clio are there too.

Leon's holding Sarah back. She's telling Char she'll fucking kill her. She's snarling, so angry she's spitting. But nothing happens.

I close my eyes tight, but Char pries them open.

"I don't want to have to use clamps. But you need to watch her."

I turn my head toward Sarah. Her eyes are bulging, and I realize that she's terrified for me. Char puts cotton in my mouth so I won't bite my tongue.

I try to smile as she turns on the machine. Immediately there's a strange and blinding pain. I have a feeling that I'm no longer in my body, that I've somehow been jarred out of myself. Like I did the night before, I see my body float outside myself, watch my arms and legs flail against the restraints.

The girl on the table looks smaller than I thought she would. The cotton in her mouth looks bloody. Her skin ripples with some unknown force, like her flesh is giving way to itself. Briefly I think that the girl I'm watching is dying, and then I think that she's being reborn. Like Orpheus, this is her second chance. But all she does is struggle against the electricity, and then the girl is back in her body.

I can feel something pulsating and buzzing inside me, making my stomach heave. I can see only blue. There's no feeling, but there's this static in my head. I try to look for Sarah, to save her, but whenever I try to hold a thought, it breaks before I can remember it. I can hear people talking, but I don't understand what they're saying, though I hear someone's name and it's mine.

Sarah's standing over me, shaking me. There's blood in my throat, and I spit out what is left of the cotton. My body feels like every bone in it has been broken. I know it's not because of Sarah, but when she puts a hand to my forehead before I put my hand over hers, I have to remind myself that she didn't do this to me.

I manage to sit up, even though my body feels like it's not there. I bring my hands up to my face, to my chest, where my heart is pumping too fast, just to make sure something is still there. Then I throw up. Soon there's nothing left but bile, vomit pooling beside me on the metal table.

Char gives me a pill and I fall asleep again.

As I lose consciousness, I think I hear Sarah saying, "When are you going to do it to me too? If she has to, so do I." And Char saying, "After I'm done treating her." Before my vision goes black, I see Leon on the now-clean table, the little wires from the machine like the tentacles of an octopus being attached to his arms, a photo of two boys kissing flickering on the screen on the wall.

***

I DREAM of her. I think Char thought she could electrocute my love for Sarah out of me, but it has only caused me to love her more. And now Sarah, too, will have her body lit up, but there's nothing I can do about it.

In my dream Sarah and I are sitting in the field we used to ride our bikes to after I'd spent the night at her house, after the nights we'd brushed our bodies together nervously, though we never talked about it. We would always wake up the next morning holding each other and pretend not to have known we were. In the dream she ties the daisies together so they create a crown and drapes them over my head. Her eyes are green in the light. This is before the boys made her cut off all her hair, when it was long and almost auburn and reached the small of her back. She tilts her head, smiles at me. She's so bright in this moment, as bright as anything when you know you're about to lose it.

"You know, I broke into a church once. It was beautiful. So cold that I could see my breath. The day before I'd kissed Bette Millie for the first time, and it had scared me so much it was like I couldn't breathe. I hadn't been able to since I kissed her. You know, I'd realized for sure that I'd loved you about a week before, though I'd felt that way for a long time. We were in the field behind the church, and you were running in circles. I don't know why, but you were. And you would wear your hair in braids then and they'd come undone, and your hair was falling all over your face like fractured rays of sun. I was scared, though, which is why I didn't say anything. I'm sorry I didn't tell you earlier; I should have. Anyway, one night my parents were gone and I was all alone in the house. My brother was out. Doing what, I don't know. So I walked to the church and I just opened the door with the spare set of keys. Raya, if you've never been in a church at night, you're lucky. It's so frightening and haunted-feeling but also beautiful. And that night, I realized it didn't have to be holy for something to be beautiful, and that's how I knew I could love you. But still, I waited for a long time to let you know until the day I kissed you. I was so scared. And I'm sorry I did it because it's what got you into this mess."

She's picking the flowers faster now, pulling the petals off their stems.

"You know, I baptized myself once. I thought it would fix me. After the night in the church, I walked to the river. It was four in the morning and nobody was awake yet. I walked in and I put my arms out and just floated for hours. I gave up the idea of being what my parents wanted me to be that night. Soon after that, sometimes when you weren't there for the night, I'd sneak out of my house when my parents were gone and sit in the quiet of the church and just think. It was the only time I felt like my father's religion could love girls like me. Like us. That's what this place is like: all those mornings in church when nobody can meet your eyes, when you're always afraid that somehow they know. I know you felt that too; I could tell. You'd grip the edge of the pew so hard you'd have bruises on your palms after service. I'd just dig my nails into my hands or sometimes grind my teeth. But I promise I'll get you out, okay?"

Then she's wearing a green dress, though I don't know why. She's gripping red flowers in her left hand so tightly they start to fall apart. She stands up, and then there's a door hanging over our heads and she turns to me. "You go first. But don't look back."

But I do look back. I do. Because she's so beautiful and I'm so scared of going somewhere without her because my whole life, even before I knew it, I've always had Sarah. And when I look back at her, she disappears and I'm alone again.

⌘ ⌘ ⌘

I WAKE up covered in sweat. Sarah's sitting on the bed next to me. "Raya? Did you hear what I said?"

"About the church?"

"No, not church. I told you that I have to do the treatment in the morning."

I move over to the end of the cot so she can move in next to me. My body aches, still. She holds me so tightly I can't breathe at first, and though I'm not sure, I think that before I drift back into the darkness, I ask her not to let me go.

⊞ ⊞ ⊞

WHEN I open my eyes the next morning, she's still holding me, her arms wrapped around my waist and her face buried in the back of my neck. Leon is grinning at us from across the room. He stands up, wearing nothing but his hot pink Speedos, and walks to the end of the room.

"Ladies, I couldn't sleep last night, so I went out and found the other rooms here, figured out where everyone's sleeping. There are three other kids. They're all roommates too. Then there's another doctor's office where Char stays if she's not outside smoking. I swiped these for us, though."

He attempts to give us three cigarettes each.

Sarah and I both shake our heads.

"More for me. If I'm going to get the shocks, I might as well take up the smoking too." He puts an unlit cigarette in his mouth and starts puffing.

"Leon?"

"Yes?" His voice is garbled, six cigarettes now dangling from his lips. "I don't think this is working."

"You need to light them."

"Ha, I know. I've been smoking since I was a cub. Can't find a lighter, though."

Leon drops the cigarettes on the floor, then shuffles back to his bed. Clio's on the upper bunk, her arm hanging over the side. Leon high-fives her before pulling the blankets over his head and curling up into himself. I hear footsteps coming down the stairs, and Sarah returns to her cot just in time.

It's Hyde, with Char behind him.

Char's holding a tray filled with steaming bowls.

"We brought your breakfast. Since everyone has physical therapy today, we wanted you all to rest."

I swallow down the lump in my throat. "How many times do we have to do the shock treatments?"

Hyde turns to me. "We call it intensive physical therapy, Raya. Usually we give you one treatment on the first day, then twice on the second day, three times on the third day, and then four times a day for two days until eventually, on the seventh day, you'll get five treatments in a row. Then you won't need treatment for a week while you recuperate. If you haven't shown signs of improving, eventually it will go up to ten rounds per session for two months. After that we evaluate it on a case-by-case basis."

I could die here. One day my body could just break down from the electricity, or worse, one day my body could become more electricity than girl. I could forget everything and never wake up from the static I felt yesterday.

At the end of the room, next to the door that connects to the room with the metal table and the machine, there's a small dining table. Char sets the tray down there.

"You know, if you want, we can bring you some of your things from the main house," she says. "Clothes, maybe. Though I think it's best for your therapy results if you don't have anything to remind you of your past life, before treatment."

My photo of Sarah and me. I want to hold it, to remind myself of everything I lost, the proof of my life before this and the proof of the other life I could have had, the life she and I could have had if everything hadn't fallen apart around us. I know that if I could hold the picture where she's looking down at me like she loves me—even though I was born with wings, even though I couldn't protect her—I would feel like everything was okay, but I don't want Char touching the picture of us. Because if she sees it or if Hyde sees it, they'll have found another weakness, and the memories I have of her before this place will always be stained with these memories. So I say nothing.

Leon asks for his socks with the silver dollars in them. When they refuse, he asks for a sweater and an extra pillow. Clio asks for the college T-shirt that they don't know belongs to the girl she left behind. Sarah asks for her blue scarf, though really the scarf is mine. I left it behind the night of the party, when everything exploded around us like a wildfire. She must have brought it with her somehow.

When they leave, Sarah turns to me.

"I didn't think I was going to see you again." She puts her hand on my shoulder, and her fingers are so cold they sting my own. I try, but I can't warm them.

🏛 🏛 🏛

GRAMMY GAVE me that scarf on my fourteenth birthday. She'd saved up for it. She would always keep little mason jars marked "for a rainy day" on the kitchen counter. The day before my birthday, when I came home from Sarah's, they were empty. At first I thought maybe we'd been robbed, but when I told her she only laughed. The next day she gave me the scarf. It was beautiful, with pale purple streaks painted in the silk. For the longest time I was scared to even wear it, and I just kept it folded up in a Ziploc bag and brought it with me everywhere I went. Sometimes I'd take it out of the bag and try it on and stare at myself in the mirror, try to convince myself that I was as beautiful as everyone told me, that I looked like somebody a girl like Sarah could one day love.

For years I was wracked with an intense guilt that Grammy had sacrificed the funds she'd been slowly saving all those years. Funds that I knew she'd always meant to keep for herself. I'd feel guilty whenever I saw her getting ready for work in the morning—pretending that she wasn't tired, that her arthritis wasn't acting up again, even when I could see her tensing her lips like she always did when something was wrong. And always—while she was at work, at church, on her long shifts, all those nights where she didn't sleep and just paced the house—I also knew that if she discovered my secret, that she would stop, that in her eyes I would be the kind of girl she could no longer love. That she'd look at me with the same disgust with which she'd looked at the two girls before they disappeared. That she'd send me away, and maybe she'd be just a little bit relieved that I was gone. Relieved because finally she could allow herself to grow old. She could stop pretending that I was her long-lost daughter, the daughter who'd left her with a kid neither of them had wanted. And she could mourn both her daughter and her husband with the kind of grief she never let herself show in front of me.

Maybe she and Paul were already married. Maybe they would start making plans to retire together and move to Florida or start a garden in the backyard. Grow tomatoes and herbs. And at night they could sit and watch all those old movies that she loved so much, and maybe, for the first time since I'd been able to remember her, she would be able to stay awake long enough to finish the movie, to be able to see it through to the end. And finally she'd be doing what she'd always thought she'd be able to do, which was exactly nothing. She could finally be a housewife and live out the quiet existence that she'd always wanted, the kind where nothing ever happens.

Looking at the scarf, I'm filled with that old sense of guilt. I wonder if Grammy even misses me. She hasn't called since she dropped me off four days ago. I think now, in her mind, I'm no longer hers. After Sarah's parents told her, she looked at me like I was nothing, like I'd never been her almost-daughter.

Char is watching us. "You girls need to have your treatments now."

I lie down on the cold metal table. Char hooks me up to the machine. As the electricity courses through my body, I try to remember snapshots of my life before: the wild roses that grow on the sides of the roads in our town. How Sarah crinkles her nose before speaking. How she forgets everything, how once she turned to me, breathless, after she'd left the stove on and had to run back to her house and said, "I'd forget how to breathe if it was possible." Though we were only thirteen, I knew right then that I wanted to spend my life remembering things for her. I remember how the houses are all lopsided and how instead of building new houses, people just add rooms onto them, so all the houses start to spread out like they're growing tumors.

But I can't stop the feeling of the electricity opening up into my body, and eventually I can feel nothing but the darkness that fills me.

The second wave of shocks rolls through my body. Then the

third. The fourth. Eventually I am conscious only of how it enters into my head and floods into me as if I were drowning in the sparking pain, as if stars have been embedded in my bones.

Then I'm sitting in one of the chairs and Sarah is being hooked into the table's straps.

Her mouth is filled with cotton pads—her arms are connected to what I think are monitors, screens with squiggly lines that I hadn't noticed before. Her body is seizing from the electricity and her eyes are rolled back so far in her head that I can see only the whites. Her legs are flailing. Spit's coming out of her mouth, and her hands are jerking against their restraints. She tries to scream, but she can't through the cotton.

I'm thinking that I need to stop this, that I need to rescue her, and I'm trying to get up. But I can't. I think at first that I'm bound to the chair and start looking for restraints, but then I realize that I'm not restrained; my body just isn't working. When I look at her jerking limbs, I feel like I'm going to get sick. I can't move my legs, and my arms feel heavy and cold, like they're carved out of ice. My limbs are still too heavy from the treatments, and when I try to throw myself out of the chair, I succeed only in moving one inch farther down the seat. I can't save her. I can't even make my body move. And so I give up on everything and decide that if I can't leave here, I might as well die here.

▨   ▨   ▨

I REMEMBER the night back in Pieria before everything fell

down around us, when Sarah was frightened and lost and beautiful in my arms, close to having everything she's ever known disappear—but not there yet. How on the night that we were found, as we ran away from the party, the moon hung so low in the sky and filled the forest with a yellow twilight.

Sometimes when I don't dream of the wings, I dream of my mother in a white bathroom at night. She's standing in front of a mirror and gripping the edges of the counter so tightly it hurts her hands. For a second in the dream I'm in her body, watching myself. I have her face, her long black hair. Then we're both crying, and though I don't know what the sadness is from, I can feel it in our bones, can feel it running through our body like a new skeleton. Then she washes her face with cold water, puts a hand to her aching stomach, and ties her pale blue silk robe tightly. She looks one last time at her now composed face and leaves. Then I'm alone in the bathroom and she's left me again.

I remember her room with the ceiling that is succumbing to mold and rot. Soon it will be falling down in strips, and eventually her whole room, the one place where I feel like I know her, will fall down. But I won't be there to mourn it.

I remember how Grammy said Paul proposed, just before everything fell apart. Maybe she's already had her quiet wedding, moved in with him and started living the quiet life she'd always wanted, the life that I'd taken away from her with my birth.

I know that while I can create new girls with new identities to pretend to be, while I can lie and destroy the girl I once was, only to resurrect her when I'm alone, I can't kill the electricity. I can't escape it. I can no longer run to my freedom. My body's too sore.

Like Orpheus, I can't save Sarah. And so for the first time in my life, I give up completely. I lie back on the cot they've moved me onto and let the dark close in on me until there's nothing left but the buzzing aftermath of electricity still humming through my bones.

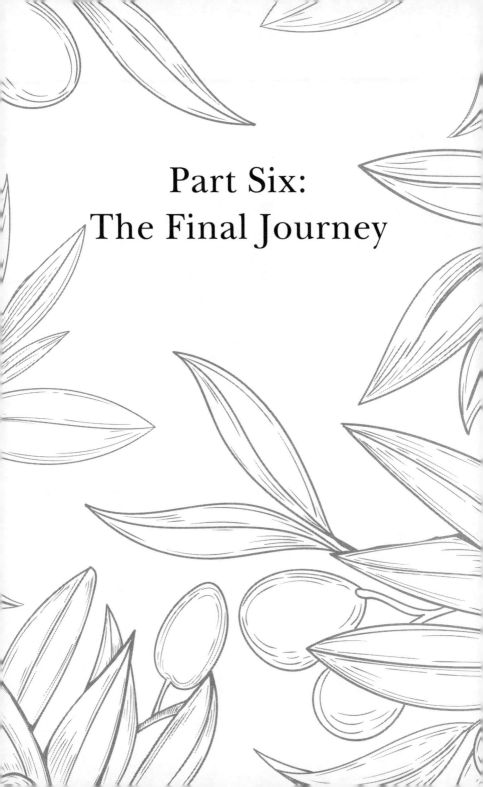

Part Six:
The Final Journey

The days blur into nothing but jolts of electricity and the gauzy feeling of cotton in my mouth. It takes me longer and longer to collect myself after the treatments, to remember the girl they're burning out of my body. Details fade. The smell of Mom's old bottle of perfume. The exact shade of gold of Grammy's cross necklace. The name of the road we took to church several times a week. Whether the girl who laughed when Aristo outed us had hair like the color of fire or the color of old pennies.

It's the sameness of the days here that makes it harder and harder to hold onto the past. I pass through them in a medicated buzz, as if I'm underwater and drowning without even realizing it. My bones are always sore. It's as if once the electricity enters me, it never quite leaves. My skin always feels like it's on fire, burning with a low, soft flame.

At night I try to wrench myself back, to remember these things: the face Sarah made when she slapped me after I first got my period. The long purple fleece skirt I'd wear in the winter. The first time it snowed in Pieria, how at first I thought the sky was falling down around me and then I felt the cold white. On that night nobody slept; we all just ran screaming through the streets with our arms held high in the air, mouths open, trying to catch snowflakes on our tongues.

The day she dropped me off here, Grammy told me she'd write, but as far as I know, she hasn't. Sometimes I think that she never intended to, that for her this was finally the way to end something she'd never wanted in the first place.

Some nights I find myself talking in my sleep. I don't know what I was saying, but I wake up to find Char, who—when not outside smoking and watching the moon—quietly paces the halls. Patrolling, making sure no one is doing anything. In a strange way this makes me feel safe, as if she were Cerberus, always there with her industrial flashlight in one hand and a bottle of water in the other.

I wake up to find her watching me, the flashlight lit up in her hand like a torch. "You were doing it again."

Every time, I say nothing, just turn my back to her. Embarrassed, even though I never know what I was saying.

But afterward she and I talk. I don't want to let her know my weaknesses. Still, gradually, I begin to tell her things. I'm just so afraid of forgetting my girlhood completely, because while I'm still a girl, I feel like I long ago passed into some-where else—into some other place, a place where girlhood doesn't exist. The therapy has done nothing for my gayness, but I no longer know the girl who was sent here.

𝌆 𝌆 𝌆

THE FIRST time I see myself is on the third day of therapy. Char brings me soap and towels and tells me that I have to shower. I'm so exhausted. Thinking about the effort it will take to shower makes me even more tired.

"I don't want to."

"You're starting to smell," she says.

When I look in the mirror, I don't recognize my face. At first I think that a stranger has somehow entered the bathroom with me. I was afraid of confronting my body, of seeing what has happened to it. The electroshock therapy leaves red marks from where she attaches the electrodes on my arms. My legs and wrists are ringed with bruises from where I'd struggled against the restraints. I've lost weight since coming here, and after the treatments I usually can't make myself eat or keep down food when I do.

In the shower I look down at my body, at the bruises from the therapy, the scars on my back that I can see only when I twist in front of the mirror—and something breaks inside my chest. I sit down on the shower floor and rock back and forth. I try to catch my breath. The cheap medicinal shampoo stings my eyes. I stay like this until the water runs cold. Then I scrub myself with a worn-down washcloth until my skin stings. I want to wash it all away: the years of shame, the circles where they tell me I am unholy, that I will never be good enough, the treatments that leave my body ablaze, changed into something that no longer feels like mine, the days spent carrying rocks. All the wasted time I'd spent hiding when I knew this would happen anyway, when I knew it was all beyond hope. I scrub my skin until my arms start to bleed.

When I'm back in my room, Char knocks on my door.

"Raya?"

I quickly struggle to put on my clothes without drying myself off, so she won't see the scratches or the strips of irritated skin, the bumps where my wings once threatened to blossom. She walks in anyway. She's brought me some new clothes. My number of treatments has gone up today. I am trying to get dressed, still wet, and I know she sees the scars, the secret that I'd tried to keep for all those years. Years where I wore one T-shirt over another to hide both my growing breasts and the vertebrae wings. I realize I'm almost looking forward to the nothing-like buzz of the aftershocks because then I won't have to grieve for anything.

🏵 🏵 🏵

HYDE COMES occasionally to check on our progress. He brings a quiz to monitor how we are doing. If we lie and say that we don't feel gay anymore, that we want to marry a man and live in a house with a white picket fence, he can tell. He threatens to up our therapy, though he never does. Sometimes I lie anyway. Tell him stories from my fake life, talk about Grammy, how I'm going to become the grand-daughter she always hoped for. Other times I just say nothing and pretend I've forgotten how to speak. Nothing ever happens. He either listens or sits there quietly when I don't talk.

After that they separate me from Sarah. They separate all of us. They take us all into small, single bedrooms.

On the first night we're separated, I think I can hear Sarah's voice rising above the buzz that is all I can hear now. But I am not sure. On the second night I try to go look for her, drag myself out of bed and start to hobble toward the door, but I can't move normally—my legs are shaking too much. Char is at the door with her flashlight. I don't know if she would stop me and I don't have enough fight left in me to find out, so I tell her I am going to the bathroom.

I lock the door and run the faucet for a few minutes.

In the mirror I see my mother's face. It is not hers, though it feels like it no longer belongs to me either. I don't remember the girl I once was. She's not the bald woman staring back—her eyes ringed with black circles, lips chapped, cuticles peeling and bloody, her ribs and collarbone protruding in ways they hadn't before.

Here she is, but where am I? I have disappeared inside my own body, and I don't know how to return. I have forgotten how to be anything but invisible, what I've been training myself to be for the entirety of my closeted girlhood. The shocks have done nothing to make me feel less gay, though they have made me supremely numb. Facts about myself have started to slip away from me. One morning I forget my birthday. Another time, my middle name. I spend half a day scouring my memory for it until I remember that it's Ava, after Grammy.

I only want to sleep because it's the one time when the soft, low hum that plagues me every waking hour is gone. I think a week has passed, though the only way I have to count this is the number of shocks I get each day. Soon the mornings begin to melt into the dark gloom that begins in autumn, and that is when Char tells me that I'm almost done with my treatments. I have one more day.

We're not allowed to close the doors except at night, so I always have to get dressed under watch. Today I sit down and hold out my arm when it's time. I stopped resisting a long time ago, after the first few treatments.

When it's over, Char smiles at me through the fog.

"You know, it's almost break. You can go home soon if you want to. Just for the break, though. We can't discharge you for a few more months, until we know that you're cured completely. You're one of the best electrotherapy patients we've had. I can't say the same for the others."

Sometimes I can't help but wonder if one day my heart will stop during one of the shock treatments. But I'm too tired to wonder that much. It's like I'm no longer in my own skin. When they first gave me the shock therapy, I'd spend the entire day experiencing the aftereffects, which make it hard to move, and then I was too spent to do anything but give in. After the first treatments, when they separated us, they moved a projector into the room, and Char makes me watch a video of two girls kissing on a gray couch during each session. Though I miss Sarah constantly, so much that it physically hurts, I'm scared of finding her, of seeing what they have been doing to her.

One night early on, Leon burst into my room. It was almost

three in the morning. He didn't say anything. I moved over so he could curl up next to me. His skin was too hot, fevered, and his body shook against mine. Eventually he spoke.

"She is okay. Not good, but she's not bad either. Is holding up pretty well. Misses you."

"I miss her too, Leon. I can't do it anymore, the fighting."

He held me closer. "You don't have to. Rest now."

I knew that wasn't true, that I should have been fighting for her. When I first came here, I told myself I was Orpheus, that I was going to get my girl and get us out of here, but I couldn't. I failed. She's still here, and I can't do anything to save her. I fell asleep next to Leon. He didn't need to say it, but I knew in that moment—though the both of us were motherless children, lost and confused with our bodies coursing with electricity—we were safe with each other.

When I woke up, he was gone, only a strand of blue-black hair on my pillow and a lingering warmth on the bed where his body was.

Char, I've learned, takes these mysterious blue pills so she doesn't have to sleep. Late at night I can sense her while I stir somewhere between sleep and semiconsciousness, and she often comes and sits with me.

Once, she apologized to me but spoke so quietly I almost didn't hear her.

The next morning I thought I'd dreamed her saying, "Raya, I'm sorry. I don't know if I can do this anymore, but I don't know what else to do, because if this entire thing was wrong, then I really lost her. I really did give her up. I've lost too much for this."

That same afternoon I tried to write Sarah a note, but my

hands shook so much my handwriting looked like chicken scrawl.

I gave it to Char anyway and asked her to bring it to Sarah. I think she did, but I don't know. Even though she's the one doing this to me, I don't hate Char. I think she's as trapped as I am, though her trap is mental. She only needs to learn how to leave.

The days still bleed together. Late at night, after my final treatment, I go to get some water and I see her in the hall, hunched over and clutching her head in her hands. The flashlight has fallen, casting shadows on the floor.

I'm thinking about going to her when she turns. I don't know if she sees me. Her eyes are unfocused. So I go back to my room, wait for her to return to herself, for the bobbing light of the flashlight to cast shadows on the walls as she paces around in the dark again. But it doesn't.

In bed I let the buzz wash over everything. Then I remember that Char told me that I'm free to leave, to go to the main house now, while I take a break between shock sessions. So I stand up. When I start walking, my knees almost give way and I start to slide to the floor. But I hold onto the wall for support and manage to pull myself up and out the door, shakily. I walk across the lawn.

Char said the shaking and the difficulty moving would go away as soon as I was done with the treatments, but so far it's only been a few hours.

Inside the house it's quiet, almost dawn.

Yesterday, in my first act of resistance in a long time, when I was in Char's old study, covered in dust and littered with outdated medical journals, I pretended to have a violent coughing fit. When Char left the room to get me water, I went through her desk drawers, looking for evidence of the girl she left behind. I wanted to understand Char's hungry look: as if she'd had spent her whole life fasting, hoping that somehow her hunger could save her. I wanted to know if it were something I could escape too. The bottom drawer was locked, but I found the key taped to the bottom of the desk and opened it.

She'd probably been told for years, like the rest of us—by our families, by our hometown preachers, by the children we grew up with—that we are wrong, that something about us is broken. She had probably been told this so many times that she believed it, or started to believe it.

If the preacher said we were wrong, that we needed to be fixed or we'd end up in hell, then our parents or our guardians would ship us off or send us back to get fixed. And no matter how many times we begged them not to abandon us, no matter how many times we'd told them that these treatments could kill us, that we were being broken, turned into something different, that we didn't know what would happen to us if things continued this way, that we didn't know what we would change into, they wouldn't listen. But still, we told them, told them we were tortured mentally and physically. That they poured hot water on our fingers, that they hooked us up to machines that electrocuted us, that they starved us. That like our older brothers and uncles and fathers who served in war and came back as shells, we too were being hollowed out.

But it didn't make a difference. Our families gave us up the moment they heard the word "queer."

One day either we wouldn't want to come back, or we would come back as someone else. But none of us ever truly returns. And this is why some of the kids cut themselves even if everything sharp has been taken from them. Why some of the kids stand in the football field and scream until they get the raspy feeling in their chests that you get from crying in the cold.

I'm always scared that my wings are coming back, that I can feel them reemerging. Sometimes I have to go to the bathroom just to check to make sure they're gone, because I swear I can feel them rustling in my spine. And the possibility of this being only in my head scares me more than the possibility that the vertebrae are growing again. Every time I twist in front of the mirror, and pull my shirt down to feel the nubby scars, I breathe a sigh of both relief and fear.

I don't know what happened with Char's family. She won't talk about anything other than the horses she once owned as a girl, before everything. Those horses are the only good memory she seems to have of her girlhood. If I want to delay or avoid therapy, I ask her questions about them and she'll go off on a jag about equestrian stuff. Sometimes she'll even talk until the end of my session without doing anything to me, and I can leave relatively unscathed. She gets this misty, faraway look, I think it's because she gave up actually being free long ago, but when she's galloping off so fast, maybe she could believe that in the moment, she could escape everything, escape the life she wasted by being held prisoner here and becoming something, someone else.

In every other aspect of her existence, though, she's given up. Like I'm beginning to.

I thought of the horses as I rifled through the drawer. I didn't have much time, but I found a certificate of graduation from the conversion program with her name on it. I already knew about that, but beneath the certificate there was a picture of a blonde girl in a high school uniform holding a loaf of bread and laughing. Her cheeks were flushed red, and by the way she looked at whoever was behind the camera, I knew that Char was the girl who took the picture and this girl was her Sarah.

My hands began to shake. Looking at her—ponytail messy around her face, smiling so wide her mouth looked all the way open, like she'd been captured in the moment directly before shouting—I felt something like hunger for the first time since the treatments. But the hunger wasn't for the girl in the photo, it was for Sarah. I wanted to hold the camera like she did in that picture, to have Sarah look through it and into me like that, to make her smile that wide.

I returned the photograph to the drawer and felt more like myself for the first time in days.

Now I'm standing at the entrance to the rec room. I see a familiar choppy head, her buzz cut framing her face like a halo. She's lying on one of the couches with her hand flung over her face.

I run to her, throw myself down at her feet, take her hand and pull it toward me. She's startled at first. I realize that she must have been sleeping. Then she grabs me and kisses me hard enough that it hurts, but not in a bad way, and I kiss her back for what feels like forever. She's holding me, running her hands over where my wings used to be, and she's crying and so am I.

Her skin hurts too; I can tell by the way she shudders when I kiss her shoulder. Later she'll say that while the shock therapy did nothing to change her gayness either, she has also started to feel hollowed out, her body consumed by a strange burning. Char has told us both that we may experience it for years after the treatments have stopped.

The burning often wakes us in the middle of the night, and we stumble to the bathroom to drink the lukewarm water straight from the tap, convinced in our dreaming haze that the burning is because our throats, our bodies, are catching fire. Sometimes we begin to shake uncontrollably, but other times our limbs grow numb and it takes us hours to be able to feel them again. After one of my first treatments, I couldn't feel my right arm for three days. Sometimes my skin hurts like something in me is teething, like my body is changing in ways beyond my control.

"I'm sorry I didn't find you. I was too scared."

She looks at me. "Don't be. Don't. Okay?"

I nod, say yes, though we both know I don't mean it. I settle in next to her with my head resting against her chest.

That's when I see Mom.

The rec room TV is almost never on, and when it is, they usually play old movies, but there she is: my mom. She's wearing a dress with a train attached to it that makes it look like she's underwater, and her eyes are rimmed with sparkling flecks of gold. For a second I think she's looking at me. Then she turns to the man on the TV who'd just tried to stab her.

"You can't kill me," she says. "I just come back."

She has a knife in one hand and a torch in the other. I know now that I can fight this, and for the first time since I got lost in hell, I realize that I can still escape.

Sarah lets me go. Puts a hand over her eyes. "Raya? I don't feel good."

"What's wrong?"

Her face is gaunt, and her body is shaking even though the house is warm. I notice that her ribs are sticking out through her T-shirt.

"I couldn't eat much for a few days, until I got too sick for the treatments and they had to stop." She starts to cry. "I was just so scared, Raya. I thought I was going to die, it hurt so much."

I don't know what to say. I should have saved her. I should have refused the treatments. Should not have crashed the truck that night. Should have run faster. Should never have let her end up here in the first place.

I catch her hands in mine. "I'm going to stop this, okay?"

She nods, then curls up in my lap, falls asleep. I think about how to get out of here: maybe if I set something outside the counselors' quarters on fire, they'd be forced to extinguish the flames before running after us and everyone would be able to escape. I could find Leon and Clio and tell everyone first so they'd have a head start. I can feel something inside myself that they broke coming back together.

After we were taken to the second house and the days became indistinguishable from one another, we slept so much that it was like we were awake the whole time. The only difference between night and day were the cracks of light seeping through the bathroom window and into the hall. We were like the lab animals I'd read about, like rats that are trained to wake only when the fluorescent lights are shining down on them.

But here, in the light, I think I can finally wake up. I can find the strength to fight again.

I close my eyes to help myself think and drift off to sleep.

I wake up to screaming. Char is standing over us, crying. Her face is twisted up and her hands are fluttering around in the air like falling leaves.

It's dark. Sarah is still asleep, and Char is the only one in the room.

I stand up. "Char?" Then I see the blood that's staining her hands.

She slumps against the wall, half falls to the floor. I think at first that the blood is hers, that finally she succumbed to the sadness that I've always sensed is about to explode out of her, but I don't see any wounds.

"What did you do?"

She's shuddering, shivering so hard her teeth knock against each other and make an eerie clicking noise.

Hyde comes running in, his white shirt is stained red. "You two need to go upstairs, with the others."

In the moment we're both too shocked to resist. It's only after the door to downstairs is locked from the outside that we think that maybe we shouldn't have listened to them, should have gone to help whoever needed it.

⊞ ⊞ ⊞

I REMEMBER that soon after I got here, Jason turned to me and said, "Every holiday here is like the apocalypse. First there's all the crying kids who want to go home but aren't welcome anymore, at least not until they're fixed. And they're all haunted by their memories of the holidays before it all happened. I know I always think of my brother before my parents abandoned me, and how we'd spend Christmas mornings together, making coffee and breakfast for our parents, and I'd let him open my gifts for me. He's only eight, you know. And Hyde always has us pray more than usual and do extra therapy and exercise, to try to keep us from lapsing. Then sometimes, and I think this is the worst, our families call us, and though I know it's wrong and I know they do too, we beg them to take us back and say we're cured, that it doesn't matter, but they always say no. And we wait for them to call back, but they never do."

Some parents and relatives send mail, which arrives a few times a week. Afterward there are always letters from all over the South scattered around various trash cans. Once I picked up a letter from Clio's mother, begging her to reply, saying that she had no choice but to send her away. But I never got any letters from home, as if in my absence Grammy had forgotten about me and the years we spent when we were all each other had. As if I had never really existed.

The depression and the isolation surface differently in everyone at Friendly Saviors. I can see it in the hunch in their shoulders, the odd glint in their eyes, a certain hollowness to their voices, the way they move, kind of like Grammy did. Like they want to disappear inside their own bodies. Sometimes it's a quiet sadness, but it's still there: unwashed and greasy buzz cuts, the stale scent of a body that's gone too long without being clean, shoulders turned into themselves.

In the depressed kids at school, it was different: little self-inflicted bruises or other kinds of wounds. Cuticles ragged from being chewed. Chapped, bloody lips. Pale lines on their arms like the roads on a map, charting out all the various ways they've tried to escape. But here it eventually becomes a desperate numbness.

Back home I always swallowed down the pain, except for on those rare nights when I would let myself cry. I would run the shower so I could break down, could cry without Grammy hearing. Like me, most of the kids here have known they were gay their whole lives. And also like me, most of them lived in a near-constant state of terror that they'd be discovered. And like me, they were all found out before they were ready. So tonight maybe Char delivered too many shocks, or maybe someone had to carry too many boulders across that field. Or maybe they were tired of constantly breaking apart, compartmentalizing and recreating themselves. Somebody—I don't know who—gave up.

⌗   ⌗   ⌗

I TRY to swallow the lump rising in my throat. Someone got pushed too far and did something—I don't know what. And so for the first time in over a week, I feel like I'm back in my body, and I hurl myself against the door and keep throwing my body against it, even when I can feel something twinge in my shoulder.

Sarah starts throwing herself against the door too.

I hear sirens in the distance, slowly getting louder. Eventually we get the wire they'd looped over the door handle on the outside to break, and we run down the stairs.

The first thing I see is the trail of blood on the floor, the flashing ambulance lights. Char's in the corner of the room, holding herself steady against the wall.

Then we see him. Michael.

He's on a cot and his arms are covered in bandages. When I was getting treatments, I never saw him in the building, but Jason said it was because he was always alone. Since Michael had been here for a few months and wasn't showing any signs of being cured, they gave him more and more shocks. Jason told me he'd stopped speaking. I didn't believe him at first, but now I can see he was telling the truth. I try to run to Michael, but Jason holds me back.

Michael had only a foster mom, and his brother died when he was fourteen. His foster mom found him wearing his brother's old clothes one day, and after he told her, she sent him away to get fixed. He doesn't have any biological family left. His mom died when he was ten, and he never knew his dad. He's all alone. He tried to kill himself last year but it didn't work. He thought his foster mom would come for him for the holidays, but she didn't show.

He's only seventeen.

I throw myself toward him. I don't know what to do. I try to pull the blanket that slipped off the cot over him, but the ambulance attendants have arrived and push me away. I fall down on my back, hard enough that the breath knocks out of me.

I see that Michael is still breathing.

After the ambulance leaves—Hyde had jumped in to go with Michael—Sarah and I and the other lost kids find ourselves alone in the front room.

The door to the kitchen is open, and there's a reddish-brown splotch on the tiles. Char is there, but she's been crying too hard to clean it up. For the first time, everyone is angry. Their rage is a seething thing. Leon picks up a vase and throws it at the front door. It shatters, shards of glass scattering across the floor. Clio punches the wall and keeps punching it until I grab her and hold her back.

Char and Hyde broke Michael with no intention of putting him back together. They would do the same thing to any of us. Jason, for once, is perfectly still—except for the vein in his jaw, always twitching. Sarah is crying into my shoulder. In place of numbness comes a blind fury. I want to burn this place down, to swallow it in fire. But instead I wrap one arm around Sarah and the other around Jason. We stand there. I stare at Michael's blood on the floor. I realize, suddenly, that I can end this now.

I walk up to Char, who's still sobbing. "Don't clean it up. Leave it for when the cops come."

She nods. "If they're coming, it will take them a while to arrive. The EMT told me Michael's going to be okay, so maybe it will take longer if it's not a police emergency. They said they won't need to keep him more than one night, Hyde's going to call his foster mom when they get to the hospital."

🔡 🔡 🔡

AFTER THAT, we all stand together in the front room and wait. For what, I don't know.

Sarah's eyes are fluttering closed. I see that she's starting to fall. I try to catch her but can't. Leon helps me lift her onto the couch. I shake her but she won't wake up.

Terrified, I run into the kitchen to get a glass of cold water, throw it over her, and she stirs.

"What?"

I kneel down beside her. "You passed out."

She turns over. "I'm just so hungry. But I don't think I can eat."

I find some yogurt in the fridge, a spoon, and come back like everything will be okay, like a boy didn't just try to take his life. But we both know it isn't going to be okay. My hands are shaking until Sarah reaches out. She holds them steady.

"What will we do now?" she asks me.

"I don't know. Char said the police will be coming soon."

"Police?"

"Because of Michael."

I look at her, but I don't have to say anything. She already knows what I'm thinking. For now, we decide to rest on the couch in the rec room.

I fall into a deep sleep. In a dream, my wings grow back but they grow out wrong and twisted. When the feathers emerge from my back, they crack the skin open and make it bleed. The pain is terrible, and as my vision begins to blacken, I think I hear her voice, but then she's gone and I'm alone. I'm Orpheus in hell without my girl. Then I wake up.

Sarah is watching me. "Are you okay?"

"Yeah. Just had a bad dream." I rub my eyes. I couldn't have been asleep for too long since the light looks the same.

She nods, stands up and walks away, comes back with Char, who sits down next to me. "Hyde called, and the authorities will be coming in a few hours. I don't know what will happen then, but there's time for you both to get out." She speaks almost mechanically, and she's paler than usual. "This is my last chance, I mean, to make things right. To try to, anyway."

I nod. When I first thought about escaping, I thought I'd go back to Pieria, back to Grammy. Now I know I can't return. Something inside me will die if I have to go back to being invisible. I would have to pretend to be cured, return to having half-coded conversations with Grammy that always leave my heart pumping in my throat. Tonight is the night I get out. If we go home, our towns will destroy us. Towns that have already broken us down, taught us shame, sent us elsewhere to be disappeared. What do any of us have to go back to?

That's why so many patients stayed here for so long, why they didn't run, even when maybe they could have. They didn't want to return to the places that had rejected them. What chance do we have if we get sent back? At best we'll always be scared, weighed down by the knowledge of what was once our secret, afraid of our sudden visibility. We will always be watched. We will never fit among the people who were once our families and our friends. On Sundays we will dig our nails into our hands during church and leave little half-moon wounds in our palms. Like the nymphs who were turned into trees or wild animals, we will be hunted by the people we once knew. We will never be safe, never escape that feeling, at least not until adulthood or college if we can afford it. And even after we've moved on, we will still look over our shoulders. We will wake up in the middle of the night with the icy fingers of panic creeping down our spines, the half-suppressed memories of the years we've tried to forget trickling back until we eventually drown in them. We will be weighed down by all the years we've spent being hated for something we can't control. So I know now that the gray morning Grammy drove me here was the last time I would ever see Pieria.

I ask Char if I can borrow a phone. Since arriving here I've tried to call Grammy only once, but she didn't pick up.

Her phone rings, but she doesn't answer. I bite my lip and dial the number again. I know that she won't answer when she recognizes the area code flitting briefly over her caller ID.

After I try for the fifth time, I give up, go to the bathroom, and look in the mirror. Maybe I've already lost myself. Maybe it started on the day they made me carry all those boulders, or the day when I first recognized what I was. Maybe it started when I realized I needed to hide, to invent a girl other than myself and try to become her. But now after years of pretending to be other girls and inventing new personalities for myself, I don't know who I am. I can still feel the shock of electricity in my body that sparks whenever I touch my skin, and when I bring my hands to my face, it stings. After all this time, I never got to become anyone other than a girl trying to survive. A girl in love with another girl. And now I'm scared that I won't be able to keep even that.

Yesterday when Sarah reached for my hand, I could feel the electricity again, the shock that reminded me that while it isn't wrong, everyone else thinks it is, and I had to move my hand away, had to pretend not to be in pain just from her touch.

I splash cold water on my face and try to smooth down my eyebrows and arrange my features in a way that looks normal,

natural—even though in my time here I've gone feral, forgotten how to even appear to be normal. I take in my
makeup-free face, my shorn head, the bland and oversized
clothes. I look like a prison escapee, or maybe a cult member,
two things that will prevent me from passing into the real
world unnoticed.

I need to find the clothes I was wearing when I arrived
here. I think they threw them out or put them in one of the
locked filing cabinets with our medical information and
behavioral files in Hyde's office. With Hyde at the hospital,
there's no way I'm getting them back. I tie the ends of the
shirt up, try to roll up the long skirt's waist so it looks like it
almost fits me. My lips are chapped; I rub the Vaseline they
keep underneath the sink over them.

In the mirror I practice looking normal, but I can't do it.

Eventually I give up. If I'm running, I'm running. Tonight
is the night that Sarah and I will escape. I don't know what
we'll do or where we'll go, but I know that we'll be gone.

After I leave the bathroom, Char walks toward me,
holding out the phone. "Raya? Your grandmother is
calling for you."

"Raya?"

When I hear her voice, I start crying. I feel a sudden
rush of longing to go back to the way things were, when it
was just the two of us floating around the empty house. For
her to again wrap an arm around me in the car on the way
to church, her gospel faintly playing in the background.

"Raya, look, I'm sorry I didn't call. I just thought it would
be too painful, for the both of us." I can hear her voice catch.
"Paul and I got married. At the church. I wore the scarf you
gave me. I wish you could have been there."

"You do?"

"Yes. I wish you could have been at the wedding." She sounds surprised.

"You should have waited for me. To get back, I mean."

"Oh, Raya." She says it quietly, but the way she says it, I know she never intended for me to come back. It hurts me more than I'd like to admit.

"You didn't think I was coming back." But it's not a question. I already know the answer.

She's quiet for a long time before she says, "Did they help at least, you know, with the problem?"

I'm silent.

"I just couldn't raise a dyke." She almost whispers it.

"Why? What's so wrong with being a dyke?"

"Oh, Raya. It's because you can't see what's wrong with it that you're so sick. It's my fault; I should have known sooner. I just didn't want to believe it. You always were so pretty, like your mother, and you seemed happier than she did. Didn't seem like you got as much of her wildness. I thought I was getting a second chance to get a girl, to raise her right. I failed your mom, honey. I didn't want to fail you like that too. I thought I could save you. The lady on the phone said something had happened, but Friendly Saviors isn't that bad, is it?"

"It is. That bad."

She sighs. "Well, there are other places. I'll look into it tonight. I'll ask Preacher Sam where he's going to send Sarah now, and then I'll come get you tomorrow. You can stay at home for the weekend, until I figure out the best place for you. We're going to get you help, okay?"

I hang up the phone and hand it back to Char. Then I sit down on the floor in the hall. I don't want to cry anymore, so I bite the inside of my cheek until my mouth fills with blood.

A tear lands on the back of my hand. Then another. I wipe them both away.

Char waves over Jason and Diane, and they crouch beside me. "Everyone who wants to is getting out tonight," Char says. "It might be the last chance you'll have before you get sent home." I stare in shock as she goes into the kitchen and comes back with an armful of plastic bags that she tosses in front of us. "Put your things in these."

She turns to me. "I couldn't get the others to leave. They wouldn't go, said they'd rather wait for their families."

For a second I see her as a girl, before she half disappeared. I see her smiling at the girl she loved, light reflecting off her face, blinding. I see her arms, years before mine, too, were covered in red marks. I see Sarah and me, wherever we end up going—lost and alone, yes, but together, free. Still ourselves. With the bright promise of a future away from here, the promise of a future for girls like us. I see Char again, laughing, the camera in one hand, her schoolbag in the other—the girl she was in that photo before she was turned against her own body, before she became something else entirely. But then I blink and the image is gone.

Leon comes running up to me. "I'm leaving, Rainy. I called my father and he wants me to come. Tonight. New York where he is stationed. Clio will turn eighteen next week, so we leave together. She'll go back to school. Find her girlfriend. Jason and Diane are coming to the station, but I don't know where they go."

I think about their escaping, finally being free for the first time, and I can't speak.

He hugs me. "Don't cry, Rainy. We'll come find you too. Everyone's leaving. Where are you going?"

I shake my head, and after a moment I collect myself and step away. "Sarah and I, our families want to send us to another camp. We're running. But I don't know where."

Leon whispers in my ear, "Come to New York with us. We'll have place for you, always." He hands me a piece of paper. "It's my phone. Call me when you get there."

I put it in my pocket. Then he slips something heavy into my hand, and when I look down, I see one of the socks with the silver dollars in it. I hug him back, hard enough that the electricity sparks in my skin and I know he can feel the wing scars through my shirt, though he says nothing and for once I don't care.

Before he goes upstairs to pack, he leans down. "You know, the thing about family is that you can choose it. And I choose you."

Only after he goes do I realize that he had tears in his eyes. Clio hugs me too, so tight it hurts. She's crying and I wipe away her tears with my sleeve.

"We'll come find you, okay?" I say. "We're getting out tonight. We'll take a bus to New York and meet you both there."

She nods. "Okay."

Char drives them to the bus station, and Sarah and I watch them leave from the porch. We go upstairs to our room. For the third time since we've been here, we pack to escape. But this time I know we will, that we're getting out. Char couldn't fit everyone in the truck, but she said she'd come back for us, and I think I believe her.

By the time Char comes back from the station, it's late, and already the air is cold against my skin. In the muddy porch light, Sarah looks at me.

For a second she's illuminated, I remember the night that we lost everything we'd known. Remember the nights as girls when we chased the dimming lights of fireflies, cupping their tiny bodies between our palms, how their wings flickered like heartbeats. And now, I see a new future for the both of us playing out in her eyes.

"I don't have time to take you two to the station, so here's the keys to the truck." Something between a laugh and a sob rises in Char's throat. "Don't crash it this time. We just got it back from the shop. It's too late for me, but you still have a chance. I'm sorry, for everything. Really. I just tried for so long."

She starts to cry, quietly. In the moonlight she looks transparent, ghostly.

I tell her, "You can still find her again. Some things can't be lost." I think, for a second, that she can come with us, that she'll get her last, small chance at redemption, become somebody, become whole, no longer a broken girl who got turned into a fractured woman.

She just sighs. "It's too late for that." Then, almost as if speaking to herself, she says, "I still love her." She blinks. "Her name was Ariana. Sometimes I think you look like her, back when we were young."

Sarah and I just stand there for a moment, but then she pushes us away.

"You're running out of time."

As I begin to walk away, I want to tell her something, to comfort her, but I don't know what to say, and by the time I realize I should have said thank you, we're running and she's only a pale shape receding into the night—her face blurred with a grief I cannot understand, her cigarette burning, wisps of smoke filling the air around her. Then I see her stand up, brush her hair down from its clip with shaking hands, and wait for whatever ending will come next for her. Darkness envelops her like a shroud. I know this will be the last time that I ever see her.

Though she hurt us, I don't blame Char. I know that she was broken, that if we'd stayed here as long as she did, we would have died or turned out the same way. We would have become the people who hated us.

I think about Grammy. She'll be waking up in a few hours to make her too-sweet coffee. She'll be tying her long gray hair up in a bun. Now that Paul is there, she'll take the time to smear on some lipstick—though like it always does, it will catch on her thin lips and smear into a pink streak on her front teeth. And like always, she won't wipe the stain away. Maybe she'll think about me. Maybe she'll wonder if she made the right choice. She'll think about how after the early shift at the florist's, she'll drive out to get me. She'll recite the words from the brochure of whatever facility she wants to send me to now. Remind herself that she's fixing me, that it's not her fault. In her mind I won't be me, though. It will be my mother she's fixing, and in her mind, if I don't come back, that'll be okay too. Because to her I've been gone for fourteen long years already.

The real me will never be hers, so she can give me away without a second thought.

Maybe my mom is waking up now too, or just getting in from some party. She'll take off her heels, tie her hair back. Maybe she'll look at the stars. Maybe she'll remember the mother and the daughter she left behind, and maybe she'll feel something sharper than sadness echoing in the space between her heart and her rib cage. But she'll do nothing, having ignored it for so long. Maybe it has already disappeared entirely.

Sarah's family will be getting ready to send her away too. They'll be sleeping still. I imagine Sarah's mom turning over, her chest hurting with what she thinks of as the death of her daughter, as if Sarah's already gone. Her daddy will think about the lessons he's been learning since he was a boy about girls like us. And though it's his own daughter, he'll think that maybe she never was anything but a broken queer he couldn't save, and his mouth will fill with a sharp, sweet taste that he can't name.

When they find out we're gone, they won't be surprised. They'll think we ended up wherever all the queers go, dead in a lake somewhere or sleeping in a car in some city. Or if we're lucky, at another one of the facilities that they try not to think about sending us to, clinging to the fantasy that these camps will fix us, that we'll become the girls they couldn't force us to be. When they sleep they'll dream of whole girls, of the girls they always wanted: straight girls who walk a certain way, who wear skirts and sing and cook and speak with a lilt in their voice. Decades of disappointments leading up to and accumulating inside the bodies of teenage lesbians like us. So for them, when we're gone, it will be a relief. One final disappointment versus a lifetime of small ones. Some nights after we leave, they'll remember when we were young, before we became something they couldn't control, and they'll feel something hollow in their chests.

The night air is cold on my skin, the skin that still burns like I'm being lit up again. We start to slow down now that we're closer, Sarah and I. And this time I don't look back. We get in the truck, lock the doors. The key slides into the ignition and the truck starts easily. I manage to steer it out into the road, and then we're driving away.

The road goes on and on. For a while I think we're never going to escape—that like Eurydice, the two of us will be trapped in hell forever.

But then the forest ends and the road opens up before us.

We'll go to New York to find Leon and Clio. Nobody will bother trying to find us. We're just gay girls whose bodies became thin air—like all the other gay kids we grew up with. We have vanished. Yet for the first time in both of our lives, we're visible by choice. And we're completely free.

As I pick up speed, I see the flash of lights in the distance, hear the faint wail of sirens, and when we get to the end of the road and onto the interstate, I see the police cars making their way down the long road to the house, and I know that it's over.

The sun starts to rise. It's almost light now. I park the truck at the edge of the road, leave the keys on the dashboard.

We grab our bags. The bus station is in the distance, with buses we could take to other cities, other states, to trains we could ride until we no longer know anything about where we are other than that we have succeeded: the two of us were gone. The expanse of road is stretching before us now, the sun's rising high, the hell we'd escaped being washed out of our clothes with its light.

Maybe I was wrong about my wings. I think that maybe the myth about Orpheus isn't about losing your love: it is about learning how not to look back.

For a minute, as we begin to walk into the sunlight, I see the two of us like we've always been—for thousands of years, since the beginning of time: two girls in the sun, their faces blurring into nothing but brightness as they leave, as they walk into the light, leaving everything behind.

Index of Characters

I've included an index of the characters in the book and their corresponding mythological references:

Raya: Orpheus.

Sarah: Eurydice, a nymph and Orpheus's wife, whom Orpheus tried to bring back from the underworld after her death.

Raya's mother, Calli: The muse Calliope, patron of epic poetry and Orpheus's mother.

Raya's father: Like Raya, the identity of Orpheus's father was disputed, but most often he was thought to be Apollo.

Jean: Artemis, the goddess of the hunt.

Madison, Sherry, and Lacey: The Three Graces, who represent beauty, elegance, and joy.

Aristo: Aristaeus, a minor god often credited with the discovery of beekeeping.

Hyde: Hades, the god of the dead and king of the underworld.

Char: Char represents both Charon and Cerberus. Charon is the ferrier for the underworld who brings the dead souls into the depths of the underworld. Cerberus is a three-headed dog who guards the underworld for Hades and prevents the dead from leaving.

Clio: Clio (also sometimes spelled Kleio) is the muse of history.

Michael: Meleager, a hero, and one of the Argonauts.

Jason: Jason, a mythological hero and the leader of the Argonauts. In their quest to recover the golden fleece, Jason journeyed with Orpheus as a member of the Argonauts.

Diane: Dysis, the goddess of the sunset who presides over the eleventh hour in the day.

Leon: Orion, a huntsman in Greek mythology.

Karma: Karmanor, the demigod of the harvest.

Raya's hometown, Pieria: Orpheus's hometown and later burial place.

Acknowledgments

I want to thank my literary agents, Vicky Bijur and Alexandra Franklin, for believing in this book and for their advocacy and literary stewardship. Thank you to Daniel Ehrenhaft and everyone at Soho Press for bringing this novel into the world. Many thanks to Bronwen Brenner and everyone else who read early drafts of *Orpheus Girl*.

Thank you to my mother, for being my closest friend and co-conspirator. And thank you to my father, for being my first reader and biggest supporter. Lastly, thank you to all the young gay people reading this. I wrote this book for you.